Frank Richard Stockton

Amos Kilbright

His Adscititious Experiences, etc.

Frank Richard Stockton

Amos Kilbright
His Adscititious Experiences, etc.

ISBN/EAN: 9783744708623

Printed in Europe, USA, Canada, Australia, Japan

Cover: Foto ©Raphael Reischuk / pixelio.de

More available books at **www.hansebooks.com**

AMOS KILBRIGHT

HIS ADSCITITIOUS EXPERIENCES

With Other Stories

BY

FRANK R. STOCKTON

NEW YORK

CHARLES SCRIBNER'S SONS

1888

TROW'S
PRINTING AND BOOKBINDING COMPANY,
NEW YORK.

CONTENTS.

*** The story of Amos Kilbright first appeared in *America*, April, 1388.

AMOS KILBRIGHT: HIS ADSCITITIOUS EXPERIENCES.

AMOS KILBRIGHT: HIS ADSCITITIOUS EXPERIENCES.

[*This story is told by Mr. Richard Colesworthy, an attorney-at-law, in a large town in one of our Eastern States. The fact that Mr. Colesworthy is a practical man, and but little given, outside of his profession, to speculative theorizing, adds a weight to his statements which they might not otherwise possess.*]

IN the practice of my profession I am in the habit of meeting with all sorts and conditions of men, women, and even children. But I do not know that I ever encountered anyone who excited in me a greater interest than the man about whom I am going to tell you.

I was busily engaged one morning in my office, which is on the ground floor of my dwelling and opens upon the street, when, after a preliminary knock, a young man entered and asked leave to speak with me. He was tall and well made, plainly but decently dressed, and with a fresh, healthy color on his smoothly shaven face. There was something in his air, a sort of respectful awkwardness, which was not without a suggestion of good

breeding, and in his countenance there was an
annoyed or troubled expression which did not sit
well upon it.   I asked him to take a chair, and as
he did so the thought came to me that I should
like to be of service to him.   Of course I desire to
aid and benefit all my clients, but there are some
persons whose appearance excites in one an in-
stinctive sympathy, and toward whom there arise
at first sight sentiments of kindliness.   The man
had said almost nothing; it was simply his manner that had impressed me.   I mention these
points because generally I do not take an interest
in persons until I know a good deal about them.

"What can I do for you ? " I asked.

The man did not immediately answer, but began searching for something in one of the pockets
of his coat.   The little awkwardness which I had
first noticed, now became more apparent.   He appeared to be looking for his pockets rather than for
what might be in one of them.   He was conscious
of his ungainliness and reddened a little as he
fumbled on the inside and outside of his coat.

"I pray you pardon me," he said, "but I will
bring before you instantly the matter of my business."

And so saying, he got his hand into a breast
pocket and drew out a little packet.   There was

a certain intonation of his voice which, at first made me think that he was not an American, but in that intonation there was really nothing foreign. He was certainly a stranger, he might be from the backwoods, and both his manner and speech appeared odd to me; but soon I had no doubt about his being my countryman. In fact, there was something in his general appearance which seemed to me to be distinctively American.

"I came to you, sir," he said, "to ask if you would have the goodness to purchase one or more of these tickets?" And he held out to me a card entitling one person to admission to a séance to be given by a party of spiritualists in one of the public buildings of the town.

A feeling of anger arose within me. I was chagrined to think that I had begun to interest myself in a person who merely came to interrupt me in my business by trying to sell me tickets to a spiritualistic exhibition. My instant impulse was to turn from the man and let him see that I was offended by his intrusion, but my reason told me that he had done nothing that called for resentment. If I had expected something more important from him, that was my affair. He had not pretended to have any other business than that which brought him.

And, besides, he offered me something which in fact I wanted. I am a member of a society for psychical research, which, about a year before, had been organized in our town. It is composed almost exclusively of persons who are desirous of honestly investigating the facts, as well as theories, connected with the spiritual phenomena, not only of our own day, but of all ages. We had heard of the spiritualistic exhibitions which were to be given in our town, and I, with a number of my fellow-members, had determined to attend them. If there was anything real or tangible in the performances of these people we wanted to know it. Considering all this, it would be foolish for me to be angry with a man who had brought me the very tickets I intended to buy, and, instead of turning away from him, I took out my pocket-book.

"I will take one ticket for each of the three séances," I said. And I placed the money on the table.

I should have been glad to buy two sets of tickets ; one for my wife ; but I knew this would be useless. She did not belong to our society, and took no interest in its investigations.

"These things are all tricks and nonsense," she said. "I don't want to know anything about them. And if they were true, I most certainly would not want to know anything about them."

So I contented myself with the tickets for my own use, and as the man slowly selected them from his little package, I asked him if he had sold many of them.

"These you now buy are the first of which I have made disposal," he answered. "For two days I have endeavored to sell them, but to no purpose. There are many people to whom I cannot bring myself to speak upon the matter, and those I have asked care not for these things. I would not have come to you, but having twice passed your open window, I liked your face and took courage."

I smiled. So this man had been studying me before I began to study him; and this discovery revived in me the desire that he had come on some more interesting business than that of selling tickets; a thing he did so badly as to make me wonder why he had undertaken it.

"I imagine," said I, "that this sort of business is out of your line."

He looked at me a moment, and then with earnestness exclaimed : "Entirely! utterly! absolutely! I am altogether unfitted for this calling, and it is an injustice to those who send me out for me to longer continue in it. Some other person might sell their tickets ; I cannot. And yet," he said, with a sigh, "what is there that I may do ?"

The idea that that strong, well-grown man should have any difficulty in finding something to do surprised me. If he chose to go out and labor with his hands—and surely no man who was willing to wander about selling tickets should object to that—there would be no difficulty in his obtaining a livelihood in our town.

"If you want regular employment," I said, "I think you can easily find it."

"I want it," he answered, his face clouded by a troubled expression, " but I cannot take it."

"Cannot take it !" I exclaimed.

"No," he said, "I am not my own master. I am as much a slave as any negro hereabouts!"

I was rather surprised at this meaningless allusion, but contented myself with asking him what he meant by not being his own master.

He looked on the floor and then he looked at me, with a steady, earnest gaze. "I should like well to tell you my story," he said. "I have been ordered not to tell it, but I have resolved that when I should meet a man to whom I should be moved to speak I would speak."

Now, I felt a very natural emotion of pride.

My perception of objects of interest was a quick and a correct one. " Speak on," I said, " I shall be very glad to hear what you have to say."

He looked toward the open door. I arose and closed it. When I had resumed my seat he drew his chair closer to me, leaned toward me, and said :

" In the first place you should know that I am a materialized spirit."

I sat up, hard pressed against the back of my chair.

"Nay, start not," he said, " I am now as truly flesh and blood as you are ; but a short three weeks ago I was a spirit in the realms of endless space. I know," he continued, "that my history is a sore thing to inflict upon any man, and there are few to whom I would have broached it, but I will make it brief. Three weeks ago these spirit-ualists held privately in this town what they call a séance, and at that time I was impelled, by a power I understood not, to appear among them. After I had come it was supposed that a mistake had been made, and that I was not the spirit wanted. In the temporary confusion occasioned by this supposition, and while the attention of the exhibitors was otherwise occupied, I was left exposed to the influence of the materializing agen-

cies for a much longer time than had been intended ; so long, indeed, that instead of remaining
in the misty, indistinct form in which spirits are
presented by these men to their patrons, I became
as thoroughly embodied, as full of physical life
and energy, and as complete a mortal man as I
was when I disappeared from this earth, one hundred and two years ago."

"One hundred and two years !" I mechanically
ejaculated.   There was upon me the impulse to
get up and go where I could breathe the outer air ;
to find my wife and talk to her about marketing
or some household affair, to get away from this
being—human or whatever he was—but this was
impossible.   That interest which dawned upon me
when I first perceived my visitor now held me as
if it had been a spell.

"Yes," he said, "I deceased in 1785, being then
in my thirtieth year.   I was a citizen of Bixbury,
on the Massachusetts coast, but I am not uncon-
nected with this place.   Old Mr. Scott, of your
town, is my grandson."

I am obliged to chronicle the fact that my present part in this conversation consisted entirely of
ejaculations.   "Old Mr. Scott your grandson !" I
said.

"Yes," he replied ; "my daughter, who was but

two years old when I left her, married Lemuel
Scott, of Bixbury, who moved to this town soon
after old Mr. Scott was born. It was, indeed,
on account of this good old man that I became
materialized. He was present at the private
séance of which I have spoken, and being asked if
he would like to see a person from the other world,
he replied that he should be pleased to behold his
grandfather. When the necessary influences were
set to work I appeared. The spiritualists, who,
without much thought, had conceived the idea
that the grandfather of old Mr. Scott ought, in
the ordinary nature of things, to be a very venera-
ble personage, were disappointed when they saw
me, and concluded I was one who, by some mistake,
had been wrongfully summoned. They, therefore, set me aside, as it were, and occupied themselves with other matters. Old Mr. Scott went
away unsatisfied, and strengthened in his disbelief
in the powers of the spiritualists, while I, as I
have before said, was left unnoticed under the power of the materializing force, until I was made
corporeal as I am now. When the spiritualists
discovered what had happened they were much dis-
turbed, and immediately set about to dematerialize me, for it is not their purpose or desire to cause
departed spirits to again become inhabitants of

this world. But all their efforts were of no avail.
I remained as much a man as anyone of themselves. They found me in full health and vigor,
for I had never had a day's sickness in my life,
having come to my death by drowning while
foolishly swimming too far from land in a strong
ebb tide, and my body, being carried out to sea,
was never recovered. Being thus put to their
wit's end, they determined to keep the matter
privy, and to make the best of it, and the first
necessity was to provide me with clothing, for on
my second entrance into this world I was as totally
without apparel as when I first came into it.
They gave me these garments of the ordinary
fashion of the day, but to which I find myself
much unaccustomed, and enjoined upon me to
keep silent in regard to what had happened ; fear-
ing, as I was made aware by some unguarded
words, that their efforts to dematerialize me might
bring them into trouble."

My professional instincts now came to the front.
"That would be murder," I said, "and nothing
less."

"So I myself told them," he continued, "for I
had come to the determination that I would choose
to finish out the life I had broken off so suddenly.
But they paid little heed to my words and con-

tinued their experiments. But, as I have told you, their efforts were without avail, and they have ceased to make further trial of dematerialization. As, of course, it would be impossible to keep a full-grown man for any considerable length of time secluded and unseen, they judged it wise to permit me to appear as an ordinary human being; and having no other use to which they could put me, they set me to selling tickets for them, and in this business I have fared so badly that I shall restore to them these that are left, and counsel them to seek another agent, I being of detriment to them rather than profit. What may then happen I do not know, for, as I told you, I am not my own master."

"I do not understand you," I said. "If you have been, in this unparalleled manner, restored to your physical existence, surely you are free to do as you please. What these spiritualists have done for you was done by accident. They intended you no benefit, and they have no claim upon you."

"That is true," he said, with a sigh, "but they have a hold upon me. It was but yesterday that they informed me that, although, so far, they had failed to restore me to what they call my normal spiritual existence, they had every reason to believe that they soon would be able to do so.

A psychic scientist of Germany has discovered a process of dematerialization, and they have sent to him for his formula. This, in a short time, they expect to receive, and they assure me that they will not hesitate to put it in force if I should cause them trouble. Now, sir," he continued, and as he spoke there was a moisture about his eyes, "I am very fond of life. I have been restored to that mortality from which I was suddenly snatched by the cruel sea, and I do not wish to lose it again until I have lived out my natural term of years. My family is one of long life, and I feel that I have a right to fifty more years of existence, and this strong desire for the natural remainder of my life is that which gives these men their power over me. I was never a coward, but I cannot but fear those who may at any moment cause this form, these limbs, my physical state and life, to vanish like a candle-flame blown out."

My sympathies were now strongly aroused in behalf of the subject of these most extraordinary conditions. "That which you fear must not be allowed," I said. "No man has the right to take away the life of another, no matter what plan or method he may use. I will see the spiritualists, and make it plain to them that what they threaten they cannot be allowed to do."

The man arose. " Sir," he said, " I feel that I have truly found a friend. Whatever may happen to me, I shall never forget your kindness to a very stranger." He held out his hand, and I stood up by him and took it. It was as much a flesh and blood hand as my own.

" What is your name?" I asked. " You have not yet told me that."

" I am Amos Kilbright, of Bixbury," he answered.

" You have not revisited your native place?" I said.

" No," he replied. " I much desire to do so, but I have no money for a journey, even on foot, and I doubt me much if those men would suffer me to go to Bixbury."

" And have you spoken to your grandson, old Mr. Scott?" I said. " It is but right that you should make yourself known to him."

" So have I thought," he answered, "and I have felt an earnest drawing toward my daughter's child. I have seen him thrice, but have not had the heart to speak to him and declare myself the progenitor of that mother whose memory I know he cherishes."

" You shall make yourself known to him," I said. " I will prepare the way."

He shook me again by the hand and took his leave without a word.   He was deeply affected.

I reseated myself by my table, one thought after another rushing through my mind.   Had ever man heard a story such as this!   What were all the experiences of the members of the Society for Psychical Research, their stories of apparitions, their instances of occult influences, their best authenticated incidents of supernaturalism compared to this experience of mine!   Should I hasten and tell it all to my wife ?   I hesitated.   If what I had heard should not be true—and this, my first doubt or suspicion impressed upon me how impossible to me had been doubt or suspicion during the presence of my visitor—it would be wrong to uselessly excite her mind.   On the other hand, if I had heard nothing but the truth, what would happen should she sympathize as deeply with Amos Kilbright as I did, and then should that worthy man suddenly become dematerialized, perhaps before her very eyes ?   No, I would not tell her— at least not yet.   But I must see the spiritualists. And that afternoon I went to them.

The leader and principal worker of the men who were about to give a series of spiritual manifestations in our town was Mr. Corbridge, a man of middle-age with a large head and earnest visage.

When I spoke to him of Amos Kilbright he was very much annoyed.

"So he has been talking to you," he said, "and after all the warnings I gave him! Well, he does that sort of thing at his own risk!"

"We all do things at our own risk," I said, "and he has as much right to choose his line of conduct as anybody else."

"No, he hasn't," said Mr. Corbridge, "he belongs to us, and it is for us to choose his line of conduct for him."

"That is nonsense," said I. "You have no more right over him than I have."

"Now then," said Mr. Corbridge, his eyes beginning to sparkle, "I may as well talk plainly to you. My associates and myself have considered this matter very carefully. At first we thought that if this fellow should tell his story we would simply pooh-pooh the whole of it, and let people think he was a little touched in his mind, which would be so natural a conclusion that everybody might be expected to come to it. But as we have determined to dematerialize him, his disappearance would bring suspicion upon us, and we might get into trouble if he should be considered a mere commonplace person. So we decided to speak out plainly, say what we had done, and what we

2

were going to do, and thus put ourselves at the
head of the spirit operators of the world. But we
are not yet ready to do anything or to make our
announcements, and if he had held his tongue we
might have given him a pretty long string."

"And do you mean," I said, "that you and
your associates positively intend to dematerialize
Mr. Kilbright?"

"Certainly," he answered.

"Then, I declare such an act would be inhuman; a horrible crime."

"No," said Mr. Corbridge, "it would be neither.
In the first place he isn't human. It is by accident that he is what he is. But it was our affair
entirely, and it was a most wonderfully fortunate
thing for us that it happened. At first it frightened us a little, but we have got used to it now,
and we see the great opportunities that this entirely unparalleled case will give us. As he is, he
is of no earthly good to anybody. You can't take
a man out of the last century and expect him to
get on in any sort of business at the present day.
He is too old-fashioned. He doesn't know how
we do things in the year eighteen eighty-seven.
We put this subject to work selling tickets just to
keep him occupied; but he can't even do that.
But, as a spirit who can be materialized or dema-

terialized whenever we please, he will be of the greatest value to us. When a spirit has been brought out as strongly as he has been it will be the easiest thing in the world to do it again. Every time you bring one out the less trouble it is to make it appear the next time you want it ; and in this case the conditions are so favorable that it will be absolute business suicide in us if we allow ourselves to lose the chance of working it. So you see, sir, that we have marked out our course, and I assure you that we intend to stick to it."

"And I assure you," said I, rising to go, "that I shall make it my business to interfere with your wicked machinations."

Mr. Corbridge laughed. "You'll find," he said, "that we have turned this thing over pretty carefully, and we are ready for whatever the courts may do. If we are charged with making away with anybody, we can, if we like, make him appear, alive and well, before judge and jury. And then what will there be to say against us? Besides, we are quite sure that no laws can be found against bringing beings from the other world, or sending them back into it, provided it can be proved by the subject's admission, or in any other manner, that he really died once in a natural way.

You cannot be tried for causing a man's death a second time."

I was not prepared to make any answer on this point, but I went away with a firm resolution to protect Amos Kilbright in the full enjoyment of his reassumed physical existence, if the power of law, or any other power, could do it.

The next morning Mr. Corbridge called on me at my office. " I shall be very sorry," he said, " if any of my remarks of yesterday should cause unpleasant feelings between us. We are desirous of being on good terms with everybody, especially with members of the Society for Psychical Research. You ought to work with us."

" We do not work with you," I replied, " nor ever shall. Our object is to search earnestly and honestly into the subject of spiritual manifestation, and not to make money out of unfortunate subjects of experiment."

" You misunderstand us," said he, "but I am not going to argue the question. I wish to be on good terms with you and to act fairly and plainly all around. We find that we cannot make use of the dematerialization process as soon as we expected, for the German scientist who controls it has declined to send us his formula, but has consented to come over and work it on this subject himself. His en-

gagements will not allow him to visit this country immediately, but he is very enthusiastic about
it, and he is bound to come before long. Now,
as you seem to be interested in this ex-Kilbright,
we will make you an offer. We will give him into
your charge until we want him. He is of no use
to us, as he can't tell us anything about spiritual
matters, his present memory beginning just where
it broke off when he sank in the ocean in seventeen
eighty-five, but he might be very useful to a man
who was inclined to study up old-time manners
and customs. And so, if it suits you, we will
make him over to you, agreeing to give you three
days' notice before we take any measures to dematerialize him. We are not afraid of your getting away with him, for our power over him will
be all the same, no matter where he is."

" I will have no man made over to me," said I,
" and Mr. Kilbright being his own master, can
do with himself what he pleases; but, as I said
before, I shall protect him, and do everything
in my power to thwart your schemes against
him. And you must remember he will have
other friends besides me. He has relatives in this
town."

" None but old Mr. Scott, at least so far as I
know," said Corbridge, " and he need not expect

any help from him, for that ancient personage is a most arrant disbeliever in spiritualism."

And with this remark he took his leave.

That very afternoon came to me Amos Kilbright, his face shining with pleasure. He greeted me warmly, and thanked me for having so kindly offered to give him employment by which he might live and feel under obligations to no man.

I had promised nothing of the kind, and my mind was filled with abhorrence of such men as Corbridge, who would not only send a person into the other world simply to gratify a scientific curiosity or for purposes of profit, but would rehabilitate a departed spirit with all his lost needs and appetites, and then foist him upon a comparative stranger for care and sustenance. Such conduct was not only mean, but criminal in its nature, and if there was no law against it, one ought to be made.

Kilbright then proceeded to tell me how happy he had been when Corbridge informed him that his dematerialization had been indefinitely postponed, and that I had consented to take him into my service. "It is now plain to me," he said, "that they have no power to do this thing and cannot obtain it from others. This discardment of me proves that they have abandoned their hopes."

It was evident that Corbridge had said nothing of the expected coming of the German scientist, and I would not be cruel enough to speak of it myself. Besides, I intended to have said scientist arrested and put under bonds as soon as he set foot on our shores.

"I do not feel," continued Kilbright, "that I am beginning a new life, but that I am taking up my old one at the point where I left it off."

"You cannot do that," I said. "Things have changed very much, and you will have to adapt yourself to those changes. In many ways you must begin again."

"I know that," he said, "and with respect to much that I see about me, I am but a child. But as I am truly a man, I shall begin to do a man's work, and what I know not of the things that are about me, that will I learn as quickly as may be. It is my purpose, sir, to labor with you in any manner which you may deem fit, and in which I may be found serviceable until I have gained sufficient money to travel to Bixbury, and there endeavor to establish myself in some worthy employment. I had at that place a small estate, but of that I shall take no heed. Without doubt it has gone, rightly, to my heirs, and even if I could deprive them of it I would not."

"Have you living heirs besides your grandson here?" I asked.

"That I know not," he said; "but if there be such I greatly long to see them."

"And how about old Mr. Scott?" said I. "When shall we go to him and tell him who you are?"

"I greatly desire that that may be done soon," answered Kilbright, "but first I wish to establish myself in some means of livelihood, so that he may not think that I come to him for maintenance."

Of course it was not possible for me to turn this man away and tell him I had nothing for him to do, and therefore I must devise employment for him. I found that he wrote a fair hand, a little stiff and labored, but legible and neat, and as I had a good deal of copying to do I decided to set him to work upon this. I procured board and lodging for him in a house near by, and a very happy being was Amos Kilbright.

As for me I felt that I was doing my duty, and a good work. But the responsibility was heavy, and my road was not at all clear before me. My principal source of anxiety was in regard to my wife. Should I tell her the truth about my new copyist, or not? In the course of a night I resolved this question and determined to tell her

everything. When the man was merely Mr. Corbridge's subject the case was different ; but to
have daily in my office a clerk who had been
drowned one hundred and two years before, and
not tell Mrs. Colesworthy of it would be an injustice to her.

When I first made known to her the facts of the
case my wife declared that she believed " Psy-
chics" had turned my brain ; but when I offered
to show her the very man who had been materialized, she consented to go down and look at him.
I informed Kilbright that my wife knew his story,
and we three had a long and very interesting conversation. After an hour's talk, during which my
wife asked a great many questions which I should
never have thought of, we went upstairs and left
Kilbright to his work.

" His story is a most wonderful one," said Mrs.
Colesworthy, " but I don't believe he is a materialized spirit, because the thing is impossible. Still
it will not do to make any mistakes, and we must
try all we can to help him in case he was drowned
when he says he was, and that German comes over
to end his mortal career a second time. Science is
getting to be such a wicked thing that I am sure
if he crosses the ocean on purpose to dematerialize
Mr. Kilbright, he will try to do it in some way or

other, whether the poor man was ever a spirit before or not. One thing, however, is certain, I want to be present when old Mr. Scott is told that that young man is his grandfather."

Mr. Kilbright worked very assiduously, and soon proved himself of considerable use to me. When he had lived in Bixbury he had been a surveyor and a farmer, and now when he finished his copying duties for the day, or when I had no work of that kind ready for him, it delighted him much to go into my garden and rake and hoe among the flowers and vegetables. I frequently walked with him about the town, showing and explaining to him the great changes that had taken place since the former times in which he had lived. But he was not impressed by these things as I expected him to be.

"It seems to me," he said, "as though I were in a foreign country, and I look upon what lies about me as if everything had always been as I see it. This town is so different from anything I have ever known that I cannot imagine it has changed from a condition which was once familiar to me. At Bixbury, however, I think the case will be otherwise. If there are changes there I shall notice them. In a little place like that, however, I have hopes that the changes will not be great."

He was very conservative, and I could see that in many cases he thought the old ways of doing things much better than the new ones. He was, however, a polite and sensible man, and knew better than to make criticisms to one who had befriended him ; but in some cases he could not conceal his disapprobation. He had seen a train of cars before I met him, and I was not able to induce him to approach again a railroad track. Whatever other feelings he may have had at first sight of a train in motion were entirely swallowed up in his abhorrence of this mode of travelling.

"We must not be in a hurry," said my wife when we talked of these matters. "When he gets more accustomed to these things he will be more surprised at them."

There were some changes, however, which truly did astonish him, and these were the alterations— in his opinion entirely uncalled for and unwarrantable—which had been made in the spelling of the words of our language since he had gone to school. No steam-engine, no application of electricity, none of the modern inventions which I showed him, caused him the emotions of amazement which were occasioned by the information that in this country "honor" was now spelled without a u.

During this time Mr. Kilbright's interest in his grandson seemed to be on the increase. He would frequently walk past the house of that old gentleman merely for the purpose of looking at him as he sat by the open window reading his newspaper or quietly smoking his evening pipe on a bench in his side yard. When he had been with me about ten days he said: " I now feel that I must go and make myself known to my grandson. I am earning my own subsistence ; and, however he may look upon me, he need not fear that I am come to be a burden upon him. You will not wonder, sir, that I long to meet with this son of the little baby girl I left behind me."

I did not wonder, and my wife and I agreed to go with him that very evening to old Mr. Scott's house. The old gentleman received us very cordially in his little parlor.

" You are a stranger in this town, sir," he said to Kilbright. " I did not exactly catch your name— Kilbright ?" he said, when it had been repeated to him, " that is one of my family names, but it is long since I have heard of anyone bearing it. My mother was a Kilbright, but she had no brothers, and no uncles of the name. My grandfather was the last of our branch of the Kilbrights. His name was Amos, and he was a Bixbury man.

From what part of the country do you come, sir?"

"My name is Amos, and I was born in Bixbury."

Old Mr. Scott sat up very straight in his chair. "Young man, that seems to me impossible!" he exclaimed. "How could there be any Kilbrights in Bixbury and I not know of it?" Then taking a pair of big silver spectacles from his pocket he put them on and attentively surveyed his visitor, whose countenance during this scrutiny was filled with emotion.

Presently the old gentleman took off his spectacles and, rising from his chair, went into another room. Quickly returning, he brought with him a small oil-painting in a narrow, old-fashioned frame. He stood it up on a table in a position where a good light from the lamp fell upon it. It was the portrait of a young man with a fresh, healthy face, dressed in an old-style high-collared coat, with a wide cravat coming up under his chin, and a bit of ruffle sticking out from his shirt-bosom. My wife and I gazed at it with awe.

"That," said old Mr. Scott, "is the picture of my grandfather, Amos Kilbright, taken at twenty-five. He was drowned at sea some years afterward, but exactly how I do not know. My moth-

er did not remember him at all. And I must say,"
he continued, putting on his spectacles again, "that
there is something of a family likeness between
you, sir, and that picture. If it wasn't for the
continental clothes in the painting there would be
a good deal of resemblance—yes, a very great
deal."

"It is my portrait," said Mr. Kilbright, his voice
trembling as he spoke. "It was painted by Tatlow Munson in the winter of seventeen eighty, in
payment for my surveying a large tract of land
north of the town, he having no money to otherwise compensate me. He wrote his name in ink
upon the back of the canvas."

Old Mr. Scott took up the picture and turned it
around. And there we all saw plainly written
upon the time-stained back, "Tatlow Munson,
1780."

Old Mr. Scott laid the picture upon the table,
took off his spectacles, and with wide-open eyes
gazed first at Mr. Kilbright and then at us.

The sight of the picture had finished the con-
version of my wife. "Oh, Mr. Scott," she cried,
leaning so far forward in her chair that it seemed
as if she were about to go down on her knees before the old man, "this gentleman is your grandfather! Yes, he is, indeed! Oh, don't discard

him, for it was you who were the cause of his being here. Don't you remember when you went to
the spiritualist meeting, and asked to see the spirit
of your grandfather? That spirit came, but you
didn't know it. The people who materialized him
were surprised when they saw this young man,
and they thought he couldn't be your grandfather,
and so they didn't say anything about it; and they
left him right in the middle of whatever they use,
and he kept on materializing without their thinking of him until he became just what you see him
now. And if he now wore old-fashioned clothes
with a queue, he would be the exact image of that
portrait of him which you have, only a little bit
older looking and fuller in the face. But the spiritualists made him cut off his long hair, because they
said that wouldn't do in these days, and dressed
him in those common clothes just like any other
person. And oh, dear Mr. Scott, you must see
for yourself that he is truly your grandfather!"

Old Mr. Scott made no answer, but still sat
with wide-open eyes gazing from one to the other
of us. As I looked at that aged, white-haired man
and thought of his mother, who must have died
ever so long ago, being the daughter of the young
man who sat opposite to him, it was indeed diffi-
cult to believe that these things could be so.

" Mr. Scott, " exclaimed my wife, "will you not speak to him ? Will you not give him your hand ? Will you not acknowledge him as your grandfather, whose picture you have always had near you, and which, when a little boy, I expect your dear mother has often told you to look up to and try to be like ? And if you have grown old, and he has not, on account of differences in circumstances, why should that make any difference in your feelings, dear Mr. Scott ? Oh, why don't you let him take you to his heart ? I don't see how you can help it," she said, with a sob, "and you his little daughter's only child!"

Old Mr. Scott rose to his feet. He pulled down the sleeves of his coat, and gave an adjusting shake to its collar and lapels. Then he turned to my wife and said: "Madam, let us two dance a Virginia reel while your husband and that other one take the poker and tongs and beat out the music on the shovel. We might as well be durned fools one way as another, and all go to the lunatic asylum together. "

Now arose Mr. Kilbright to his feet, and stood up very tall. "Grandson Lemuel," he said, " I leave not your house in anger. I see well that too heavy a task has been laid upon your declining years when you are asked to believe that which you have heard to-day. But I wish you to know that I am here to ask nothing of you save that you will give me your hand. I earnestly crave that I may again touch one of my own flesh and blood."

Old Mr. Scott picked up the portrait and looked at it. Then he laid it down and looked at Mr. Kilbright. "Young man," said he, "can you stand there and put your hand upon your heart, and say to me that you are truly Amos Kilbright, my mother's father, who was drowned in the last century, and who was brought back and turned into a live man by those spiritualists; and that you are willing to come here and let yourself be vouched for by Mr. and Mrs. Colesworthy, who belong to some sort of society of that kind and ought to know about such things?"

I was on the point of remarking that the Society for Psychical Research had nothing to do with spiritualism except to investigate it, but my wife saw my intention and checked me.

Mr. Kilbright put his hand upon his heart and bowed. "What you have heard is true," he said. "On my honor, I swear it."

"Then, grandfather," said old Mr. Scott, "here is my hand. It doesn't do to doubt things in these days. I didn't believe in the telephone when they first told me of it, but when I had a

3

talk with Squire Braddon through a wire, and heard his new boots creak as he came up to see who it was wanted him, and he in his own house a good two miles away, I gave in. ' Fetch on your wonders,' says I, ' I am ready.' And I don't suppose I ought to be any more dumfounded at seeing my grandfather than at any of the other wonders. I'm getting too old now to try to find out the whys and the wherefores of the new things that turn up every day. I must just take them as they come. And so if you, grandfather Kilbright, and our good friends, Mr. and Mrs. Colesworthy, will come into the back room we'll have a cup of tea, and a talk over old times. To be sure, there will be some gaps which none of us will be able to get over, but we must do the best we can."

After this Mr. Kilbright and his grandson saw a good deal of each other, and the old gentleman always treated his mother's father with the respectful deference which was due to such a relative.

" There are times," he once said to me, " when this grandfather business looks to me about as big and tough as anything that any human being was ever called on to swallow. But then I consider that you and Mrs. Colesworthy have looked into these matters, and I haven't, and that knowin' nothin' I ought to say nothin'; and if it ever

happens to look particularly tough, I just call to
mind the telephone and Squire Braddon's creaking
boots, and that settles it."

Mr. Kilbright became more and more useful to
me, particularly after he had disciplined his mind
to the new style of spelling. And when he had
been with me about a month I insisted that he
should take a holiday and visit Bixbury, for I knew
that to do this was the great desire of his heart.
He could easily reach his native place by rail, but
believing that he would rather not go at all than
travel on a train, I procured a saddle-horse for him,
and when I had given him full directions as to the
roads, he set out.

In four days he returned. "How did you find
Bixbury?" I asked of him.

"There is no longer such a place," he answered,
sadly. "I found a town of that name, but it is
not the Bixbury in which I was born. That has
utterly disappeared."

And, after this, he never again alluded to his
native place.

The high character and many admirable quali-
ties of this man daily increased the affectionate
regard and esteem in which he was held by my
wife and myself; and feeling that we could do
nothing better for him than to endeavor to make

him forget the things of the past, and take a lively and earnest interest in those of the present, we set ourselves to work upon this task. In a great degree our efforts were successful, and we soon perceived that Mr. Kilbright cared more and more for what he saw about him. It was, indeed, natural that he should do this, for he was still a young man, and able to adapt himself to changes in his surroundings.

As I have said, he gradually did so adapt himself, and in the course of the autumn this adaptation took a form which at first amused Mrs. Colesworthy and myself, and afterward enlisted our hearty sympathy. He became attached to Miss Budworth, the librarian of our town library. He frequently went there for books, and as she was a very intelligent young woman, and very willing to aid him in his selections, it was not strange that he should become interested in her. Very often he would remain at the library until it closed in the evening, when he would walk to her home with her, discoursing upon literary and historical subjects.

My wife and I discussed this situation very thoroughly. Lilian Budworth was a good girl, a sensible one, and a very good-looking one. Her family was highly respectable and her years well proportioned to those of Mr. Kilbright. There seemed to be, therefore, no reason why this intimacy should not be encouraged. But yet we talked over the matter night after night.

"You see," said my wife, "it all seems plain and simple enough; but, on the other hand, it isn't. In the first place, she does not know that he has had a wife, or what old Mr. Scott is to him. He has promised us that he will never say anything to anybody about having lived in the last century without first consulting us; and old Mr. Scott has said over and over again that he doesn't intend to speak of it; and the spiritualists have left town long ago; so, of course, she knows nothing about it. But, if things go on, she must be told, and what will happen then, I would like to know!"

"I am very sorry, indeed, that I cannot tell you," I answered.

"It would be a queer case, anyway," Mrs. Colesworthy continued. "Mr. Kilbright has had a wife, but he never was a widower. Now, having been married, and never having been a widower, it would seem as if he ought not to marry again. But his first wife is dead now, there can be no doubt about that."

It was not long before there was no further need for suppositions in regard to this matter, for Mr.

Kilbright came to us and announced that he had determined to offer himself in marriage to Miss Budworth.

"I think it is meet and proper," he said, "that I should wed and take that position at the head of a family which a right-minded and respectable man of my age should fill. I reasoned thus when for the first time I took upon me this pleasing duty, and these reasons have now the self-same weight as then. I have been studying the surveying methods of the present day, and I believe I could re-establish myself in my former profession. Thus could I maintain a wife, if, happily, I get her."

"Get her!" exclaimed Mrs. Colesworthy, "of course you will get her! She can't help accepting you."

"I should feel the more hope, madam," said Mr. Kilbright, "were it not requisite that she be informed of all that has happened to me. And all this must she know before I require her to make answer to me."

"I must admit," I said, "that I am afraid you are going to have a tough job."

"I don't believe it!" warmly exclaimed my wife. "Lilian Budworth is a girl of good, solid sense, and when she knows just exactly what has happened, it is my opinion she will not object a bit."

"Madam," said Mr. Kilbright, "you greatly embolden me, and I shall speak to Miss Budworth this very day."

Notwithstanding my wife's confidence in Miss Lilian's good sense, she was as much surprised as I when, the next morning, Mr. Kilbright informed us that he had been accepted. As it was yet an hour before the library would open, she hurried around to Miss Budworth's home to know all about it.

The young lady was found, pale, but very happy. "When he left me last night," she said, "my mind was in a strange hubbub. He had told me that he loved me, and had asked me to marry him, and my heart would not let me say anything but 'yes;' and yet, after he had gone, his wondrous story came up before me as it had not come when he told it, having just told something else. I did not sleep all night, thinking of it. I have read and pondered a great deal upon these subjects, but have never been able to make up my mind whether or not to put faith in the strange spiritual manifestations of which we are told. So I determined, a good while ago, not to consider the matter at all. I could do nothing with it, and it would be better that I should let it alone. To this same determination I came early this morning in the case of Mr. Kilbright. None of us know what we may once have been, nor what we may become. All we know is what we are. Mr. Kilbright may be mistaken as to what he was, but I know what he is. And to that man I give myself as I am. I am perfectly satisfied with the present."

Mrs. Colesworthy enfolded her in an approbatory embrace, and hurried home to tell me about it. "There now!" she exclaimed, "didn't I say that Lilian Budworth was a girl of good, sound common-sense?"

"That is what you said," I answered, "but I must admit that I was afraid her common-sense would interfere with her acceptance of his story. We had outside evidence in regard to it, but she had only his simple statement."

"Which is quite enough, when a woman truly loves," said Mrs. Colesworthy.

When old Mr. Scott was informed what had happened, he put down his newspaper, took off his spectacles, and smiled a strange, wide smile. "I have been reading," he said, "about a little machine, or box, that you can talk into and then cork up and send by mail across the ocean to anybody you know there. And then he can uncork it, and

out will come all you have said in your very words
and voice, with the sniffles and sneezes that might
have got in accidental. So that if one of the Old
Testament Egyptians that they've been diggin'
up lately had had one of these boxes with him it
might have been uncorked and people could have
heard in his own voice just who he was and what
was his personal opinion of Moses and his brother
Aaron. Now, when an old man like me has just
come to know of a thing of this kind, it isn't for
him to have a word to say when he is told that
Lilian Budworth is to be his step-grandmother; he
must take it in along with the other wonders."

As to Mr. Kilbright and his lady-love they
troubled themselves about no wonders. Life was
very real to them, and very delightful; and they
were happy. Despite her resolutions to give no
consideration whatever to her lover's previous existence, Miss Budworth did consider it a good deal,
and talked and thought about it, and at last came
to understand and appreciate the fact as thoroughly
as did Mrs. Colesworthy and myself; and she
learned much more of Mr. Kilbright's former life
than his modesty had allowed him to tell us.
And some of these things she related with much
pride. He had been a soldier during the Revolu-
tion, having enlisted, at the age of twenty-three,

under General Sullivan, when his forces lay near
Newport.   He afterward followed that comman-
der in his Indian campaigns in Western New
York, and served during the rest of the war.   It
was when the army was in winter quarters in
1780 that Tatlow Munson painted his portrait
in payment of an old debt.   Miss Budworth's
glowing rendition of Mr. Kilbright's allusions to
some of the revolutionary incidents in which he
had had a part, made us proud to shake hands
with a man who had fought for our liberties and
helped to give us the independence which we
now enjoy.

Mr. Kilbright's business prospects soon began to
look promising.   As was quite natural, his ideas
upon some subjects were a little antiquated.   But,
although many of the changes and improvements
he saw about him met with no favor in his eyes,
he had sense enough to take advantage of certain
modern progressive ideas, especially such as related to his profession of surveying.   My introduc-
tion of him as a friend from Bixbury helped him
much in respect to patronage, and having devoted
all his spare time during the autumn and winter to
study and the formation of business connections,
he secured enough profitable employment for the
coming season to justify him in taking to himself

a wife; and his marriage with Miss Budworth was appointed for the middle of April.

It was about the end of March when I received a letter from Mr. Corbridge, the spiritualist manager, in which he informed me that Dr. Hildstein, the German scientist, of whom he had previously spoken to me, had set sail for America and would probably arrive in about ten days. " As soon as possible after his arrival," wrote Mr. Corbridge, " we shall resume possession of the subject of whom you have been kind enough to take charge during the time when we had no need of him. He will then be dematerialized in order that we may cause him to manifest himself in our seances whenever it may be desirable; but never, I may say, in the complete and perfect physical condition to which he was unintentionally materialized the first time. I promised you that I would give you at least three days' notice of our intention to resume work on this subject, and I have now been much better than my word. I have written very plainly of our intentions, because we wish you to understand exactly what we are going to do; and should we succeed in our proposed experiment, which we certainly expect to do, we shall, probably, make public our whole action in the affair, for this course would most greatly benefit both ourselves and our

cause. It will not be necessary for you to inform
the subject of our intention, for our power over
him will be as great at one time and at one place
as at another; and as his co-operation is not in
any way needful, you will see for yourself that it
will be pleasanter for him not to concern himself
with what we are about to do."

When I had read this letter, I sat for half an
hour with it open in my hands. It came upon
me like a shower of iced water. I had supposed
that the spiritualists had utterly abandoned their
endeavors to dematerialize Mr. Kilbright. Therefore, the news of the revival of these criminal intentions greatly shocked me. To be sure, the
coming scientist might have no such power as he
pretended to possess, but this supposition did not
comfort me. If the man had not already had success in that sort of thing it is not likely that he
would come over here to attempt it now.

When I had sufficiently quieted my mental agi-
tation I wrote instantly to Mr. Corbridge, and in
my letter I assumed a very confident tone. I told
him that Mr. Kilbright's circumstances had so
changed that the intended action of the spiritualists in regard to him was now rendered impossible. He had become an active member of society,
had gone into business, and would be married in

April. The mere statement of these facts would, I felt quite certain—so I wrote—cause the spiritualists to instantly relinquish all idea of carrying out their previous intention in regard to this most estimable man. If, however, any inhuman craving for scientific investigation should cause them to persist in their cruel and criminal designs, the utmost power of the law should be invoked against them. " To take away human life," I wrote, " in a case like this is murder, no matter how it is done, and should you take away Mr. Kilbright's life, or even attempt it, you shall be indicted and punished for this cold-blooded and premeditated crime."

Before I had read this letter, I found it absolutely necessary for my peace of mind that I should make my wife acquainted with the threatened danger, and confer with her as to what it would be well to do. Of course, Mrs. Colesworthy was greatly shocked when I read her Corbridge's letter, but she recovered courage sooner than I had done.

" It's all stuff and nonsense," she said. " The man is just as much alive as you and I are, and I don't believe any human power can turn him into a spirit. They might kill him, but then he would be a dead man and not a spiritual mist or vapor. I don't believe they even intend to try to do anything of the kind. They merely wish you to hand him over to them so they can make him work for them for little or no pay. They think, and with good reason, too, that by this time you have taught him how to get along at the present day, and that he may now be of some use to them."

I showed her the letter I had written, and she highly approved of it. " If I were you," she said, " I would send that letter, and then I would not do another thing. Take my word for it, you will never hear from those people again."

We resolved, of course, that we would say nothing to Mr. Kilbright or Lilian about this matter, for it was unwise to needlessly trouble their minds ; but we could not help talking about it a great deal ourselves. In spite of the reassuring arguments which we continually thought of, or spoke of to each other, we were troubled, anxious, and apprehensive.

" If we could only get them safely married," said Mrs. Colesworthy, " I should feel at ease. Certainly those people would not do anything to him then."

" I don't believe they can do anything to him at all," I answered. " But how a marriage is going to protect him I cannot imagine."

" Of course, you can't explain such things," said

my wife, "but I do wish they were married and settled."

Not long after this she came to me with a supposition. "Supposing," she said, "that those people find it impossible to dematerialize him, they might do something which would be a great deal worse."

"What could that possibly be?" I asked.

"They might materialize his first wife," said she, "and could anything be more dreadful than that? I suppose that woman lived to a good old age, and to bring her forward now would be a height of cruelty of which I believe those people to be fully capable."

"My dear," I exclaimed, "don't bring up any harrowing possibilities which no one but yourself is likely to think of."

"I wish I could be sure of that," she said. "I have heard, but I don't know how true it is, that spirits cannot be called up and materialized unless somebody wants them, and I don't suppose there is anybody who wants the first Mrs. Kilbright. But these men might so work on Mr. Kilbright's mind as to make him think that he ought to want her."

I groaned. "Dear me!" I said. "I suppose if they did that they would also bring up old Mr.

Scott's mother, and then we should have a united family."

"And a very funny one it would be," said my wife, smiling, notwithstanding her fears, "for now I remember that old Mr. Scott told me that his grandmother died before she was sixty, but that his mother lived to be seventy-five. Now, he is eighty, if he is a day, so there would be a regular gradation of ages in the family, only it would run backward instead of in the usual way. But, thinking it over, I don't believe the spiritualists will permanently bring up any more of that family. If they did, they would have to support them, for they could not ask old Mr. Scott to do it, who hasn't money enough to satisfy his descendants, and ought not to be expected to support his ancestors."

My letter must have had a good deal of effect upon Mr. Corbridge, for in less than a week after it was written he came into my office. He informed me that he and his associates were about to give a series of séances in our town, but that he had come on before the others in order to talk to me. "I am extremely sorry," he said, "to hear of this proposed marriage. We want to do what is right and fair, and we have no desire that any act of ours shall create a widow."

" Then," I exclaimed, " you relinquish your design against Mr. Kilbright ? "

" Not at all," said he. " We shall carry out our plan before our subject marries. If you choose to hurry up matters and have the wedding take place before we are ready to proceed with our dematerializing process, we shall be very sorry, but the blame must rest on you. You should have had consideration enough for all parties to prevent any such complication as an engagement to marry. As to what you said in your letter in regard to invoking the law against us, I attach no weight whatever to that threat."

" You will find you have made a great mistake," said I, angrily, " when I have brought the law to bear upon you, which now I shall not delay to do."

" You will merely bring ridicule upon yourself," he said, " if you assert that the man you wish to protect is Amos Kilbright. We can prove by records, still to be seen in Bixbury, that said person died in seventeen eighty-five. On the other hand, if you choose to assert that he is, or was, anybody else, how are you going to prove it ? All that you can say is that the person you refer to came from, you knew not where, and has gone, you know not where. If you declare that at one time he was a materialized spirit, you know very well how such

4

a statement as that would be received in a court of law. It will be much wiser to let it be supposed that the person who has lately been seen about this town has run off to Canada, than to make any sort of legal inquiry into the matter. If said person were really a man we could have nothing to do with his disappearance, while if he were a materialized spirit the law would have nothing to do with him."

I arose and paced the floor. There was entirely too much force in this man's arguments, but, although I could not immediately answer him, his cool determination to persevere in his iniquitous designs so angered me that I declared that he should be punished if I had to do it myself.

" Then you admit," he said, with a smile, " that the law cannot do it. The situation," he continued, "is very plain to us. Although the law can take no cognizance of our action, the case will be very different with all believers in spiritualism, and those who are interested in us. The news that we have done this thing will spread through the spiritualistic circles of the world. "

" Has your German arrived ? " I asked, abruptly.

"Not yet," answered Corbridge, "but we expect him in a few days. He will come directly to this town, because we wish to give him an opportunity of observing the subject in his present form before beginning the dematerializing process."

"What refinement of cruelty!" I exclaimed.

"Oh, of course, the doctor will not make himself known," said Corbridge. "He will merely wish to take a good look at the subject, and see for himself how perfect his materialization has been. Then he will know just what work is before him."

And, so saying, Mr. Corbridge went away, leaving me too angry to speak, if, indeed, I could have thought of anything which it would have been worth my while to say.

When Mrs. Colesworthy heard what Corbridge had said, she turned white. "They must be married instantly!" she exclaimed. "I knew that was the only way."

It was all very well to talk of an immediate marriage, but it was not so easy to bring it about. It was yet a week before the day fixed for the wedding, and the happy lovers were busy with their preparations, never dreaming of the danger which hung over them. What reason could we give for hastening the marriage rites? At one time we thought it might be wise to explain to them fully the state of the case, but from this course we were deterred for fear of the terrible effect that the news might have on Lilian. Should

she hear of the design of Dr. Hildstein, she would
never again have a moment's peace, married or
unmarried.   Once I advised that the two be dis-
suaded from marrying, at least for a year.   In that
time we could see if these people really had any
power over Mr. Kilbright.

"That will not do at all," said Mrs. Colesworthy.
"It will be very long to postpone their happiness;
and besides, if that German gets hold of Mr. Kilbright while he is still unmarried, he will snap him
up, or rather, blow him out in no time."

"I thought we had persuaded ourselves," I said,
sadly, "that no one could have any real power of
dematerialization."

"So we had," said she, "but that sort of per-
suasion does not always last."

The result was that we did nothing but hope for
the best.   But we could not blame ourselves, for,
really, there was nothing else to do.   I had given
up all idea of endeavoring to put Mr. Corbridge
and his associates under legal restriction, because
if they had power to do the evil we feared, they
could do it in one place as well as another, and no
court could determine when, how, or by whom
Mr. Kilbright had been dematerialized.

The day before the wedding-day the German
doctor arrived in our town; and, having heard this,

I went immediately to the hotel where Mr. Corbridge and his party were staying. The spiritualistic manager was not glad to see me, and frankly said so.

"I had hoped," he remarked, "that you had concluded to keep out of this thing. It is no concern of yours; you can be of no possible good to anybody; and the wisest thing you can do will be to drop it."

I assured him that I had no intention of dropping it, and that I should do everything in my power to protect Mr. Kilbright.

"Then, again," continued Corbridge, "there is really no need of giving yourself all this worry. Dr. Hildstein may succeed, and he may not. We have failed, and so may he. He has seen the subject, and has come to a very philosophical and sensible conclusion in regard to him. He will not believe, merely on our assertion, that the man is a materialized spirit. He will proceed with his experiments, and if they fail he will consider that the man is a man, and was never anything else. If they succeed, then he will be quite satisfied that he had a perfect right to dematerialize what we had materialized."

"Then you really believe," I said, "that there is a chance that he may fail?"

"Of course there is," said Corbridge. "I do not know his methods, and there may be nothing in them."

I had no doubt that this change of tone in Corbridge was intended to produce in me a feeling of security, that they might thus rid themselves of me. But, though I saw through his purpose, the man's words encouraged me. Of course there must be a good deal of doubt about the German's powers; and, after all, there might be no cause whatever for our anxieties.

"Now, sir," said Corbridge, as I left, "if I were you I would trouble myself no more about this matter. If Dr. Hildstein fails, you will still have your man to do your copying, or your surveying, or anything you like. If he succeeds, we are all in the same condition we were a year ago. 'That subject did not exist at that time; he does not exist at this time;' that will be all we shall have to say about it."

"You forget," I said, severely, "the wife he may leave behind him."

"I have nothing to say about that," said Corbridge, rather sharply. "It is a reprehensible business, and I have nothing to do with it."

I went away without seeing the German doctor, but as I heard he spoke no English, and as I did not know German, an interview with him would have been of no avail.

Neither Mrs. Colesworthy nor myself slept that night; we were so filled with anxious fears. But when the day broke, bright and clear, and I had hurried round to Mr. Kilbright's lodgings, and had found him as full of life and vigor as I had ever seen him, we were greatly comforted, and ate our breakfasts with fair appetites.

"If it had been a dark and lowering day," said my wife, "I don't believe I could have swallowed a mouthful."

The marriage was to take place at noon, and the happy pair were to start by the first afternoon train for the sea-shore, where they were to spend a week. Mr. Kilbright hated locomotives and railroads almost as much as ever, but he had told me some time before that he intended to conquer this prejudice, if such a thing were possible.

"Being one of you, I must do as you do," he had said.

The wedding was to be a very simple one. Miss Budworth was to go from her mother's house to the church, where Mr. Kilbright was to meet her. We insisted that he should dress at our house, where he would find better accommodations than at his lodgings; and we assigned him our best guest-room, where he repaired in very good season, to array himself in his wedding suit.

It was not quite eleven o'clock when I went up-stairs to see if I could be of any use to Mr. Kilbright in regard to the conclusion of his toilette. I knocked at the door, but received no answer. Waiting a few moments, I opened it and entered. On the floor, in front of a tall dressing-glass, was a suit of clothes. Not only did I see the black broadcloth suit—not laid out at length, but all in a compact heap—but I saw the shoes and stockings, the collar and cravat; everything. Near by lay a whisk broom.

The truth was plain. While giving the last touches to his wedding attire, all that was Amos Kilbright had utterly disappeared!

I stood where I had stopped, just inside the door, trembling, scarcely breathing, so stunned by the terrible sight of those clothes that I could not move, nor scarcely think. If I had seen his dead body there I should have been shocked, but to see nothing! It was awful to such an extent that my mind could not deal with it!

Presently I heard a step, and slightly turning, saw my wife close by me. She had passed the open door, and seeing me standing as if stricken into a statue, had entered.

It did not need that I should speak to her. Pale as a sheet she stood beside me, her hand tightly grasping my arm, and with her lips pallid with horror, she formed the words: "They have done it!"

In a few moments she pulled me gently back, and said, in quick, low tones, as if we had been in presence of the dead: "In less than an hour she will be at the church. We must not stay here."

With this she turned and stepped quickly from the room. I followed, closing the door behind me.

Swiftly moving, and without a word, my wife put on her hat and left the house. Mechanically I followed. I could speak no word of comfort to that poor girl, at this moment the happiest of expectant brides. I knew that I had not the power to even attempt to explain to her the nature of the dreadful calamity that had fallen upon her. But I could not let my wife go alone. She, indeed, must speak to Lilian, but there were other members of the family; I might do something.

To my great surprise, Mrs. Colesworthy did not turn into the street which led to the Budworths' house, but went straight on. I thought at first she was going to the church to countermand the wedding preparations. But before I could put a question to her she had gone around a corner, and was hurrying up the steps of the principal hotel in our town.

"Is Dr. Hildstein in?" she asked of the first person she met.

The man, gazing astonished at her pallid face, replied that he was, and immediately conducted us to a little parlor on the first floor, the door of which stood partly open. Without knocking, Mrs. Colesworthy hastily entered, I closely following. A middle-aged man suddenly arose from a small table at which he was sitting, and turning quickly toward us, made an abrupt exclamation in German.

As I have said, I do not understand German, but Mrs. Colesworthy knows the language well, and, stepping up to the man, she said (she afterward told me the meaning of the words that passed between them): "Are you Dr. Hildstein?"

"I am," he said, his face agitated by emotion, and his eyes sparkling, "but I can see no one, speak to no one! I go out this moment to observe the result of an important experiment!"

My wife motioned to me to close the door. "You need not go," she said, "I can tell you that your experiment has succeeded. You have dematerialized Mr. Kilbright. In one hour he was to be married to a noble, loving woman; and now all that remains where he stood is a pile of clothes!"

"Do you tell me that?" exclaimed the doctor, wildly seizing his hat.

"Stop!" cried Mrs. Colesworthy, her face glowing with excitement, her eyes flashing, and her right arm extended. "Stir not one step! Do you know what you have done?"

"I have done what I had a right to do!" exclaimed the doctor, almost in a shout. "If he is gone he was nothing but a spirit. Tell me where ——"

"I will tell you this!" exclaimed my wife. "He was a great deal more than a spirit. He was a man engaged to be married at twelve o'clock this day. You may think there is no law that will sweep down on you, but I tell you there is; and before the clock strikes twelve you shall know it. Do you imagine you have come upon a people who will endure the presence of an ogre? a wretch, who reduces to nothing a fellow human being, and calls it an experiment? When we tell what you have done—my husband cannot speak German, but he is a leader in this town, and he supports me in all I say—when we have told what you have done there will be no need of courts, or judges, or lawyers for you. Like a wild beast you will be hunted down; you will be trampled under foot; you will be torn to pieces! Fire, the sword, the hangman's noose, clubs, and crowbars will not be enough to satisfy the vengeance of an outraged people upon a cold-blooded wretch who came to this country solely for the purpose of perpetrating a crime more awful than anything that was ever known before! Did you ever hear of lynching? I see by your face you know what that means. You are in the midst of a people who, in ten short minutes, will be shrieking for your blood!"

The man's face changed, and he looked anxiously at me. I did not know what my wife had been saying, but I had seen by her manner that she had been threatening him, and I shook my uplifted fist.

"Now heed what I say," cried Mrs. Colesworthy, "if you do not wish to perish at the hands of an infuriated mob; to die a thousand deaths before your vile spirit leaves this world, knowing that, besides the torments you feel, and those which are to come, you will be in the power of men who will bring you back in a half-finished form to make sport at their meetings whenever they feel like it——"

Drops of perspiration stood on the doctor's face.

" Stop that ! " he cried, throwing up his arm. " I cannot stand that ! I did not know the subject had such friends ! "

" Nothing shall be stopped ! " exclaimed my wife, " and everything shall happen unless you immediately sit down at that table, or wherever you do those things, and rematerialize Mr. Kilbright, just as you found him, and into the very clothes that were left lying upon the floor ! "

The doctor stepped forward—his face was now pale—and addressed himself very deferentially to my wife, totally ignoring me. " If you will retire," he said, " I will try ; I swear to you that I will try."

" There is not a minute to be lost," said Mrs. Colesworthy, " not one second. And, if as much as a finger-nail is missing, remember what I have told you ! "

And with this we quickly left the room.

As we went down the steps of the hotel Mrs. Colesworthy looked at her watch. " It is twenty-five minutes to twelve," she said. " We must get home as fast as we can."

We hurried along, sometimes almost running. When we reached our house, Mrs. Colesworthy motioned to me to go upstairs. She had no breath left with which to speak. I ran up, and stood for a moment at the closed door of our guest-room. With my hand on the knob, I was unable to open it. I heard a step on the stairs behind me, and I opened the door.

There stood Mr. Kilbright in his wedding clothes, with the whisk-broom in his hand.

He turned at the sound of my entrance.

"Do you know," cried the cheery voice of my wife, from just outside the door, "that we have barely fifteen minutes in which to get to the church?"

"Can that be?" cried Mr. Kilbright. "The time has flown without my knowing it. We must truly make haste!"

"Indeed we must," said Mrs. Colesworthy, and as she stepped back from the door, she whispered in my ear: "Not a look, not a tremble to let him know!"

In less than thirty seconds we were on our way to the church, in the carriage which had been ordered for the purpose.

On the church porch we found old Mr. Scott. He was dressed in his best clothes, and greeted us cordially. "In good time," he said. "I am glad to see that. It promises well." And then, looking around to see that no one was within hearing, he came nearer to us. "If I were you," he continued, "I wouldn't say nothin' to folks in general about relationships, for there are people, and very good people, too, whose minds haven't got on far enough to make 'em able to understand telephones and the other new kinds of wonders."

We acknowledged the force of his remarks, and all went into the church.

Three days after the departure of Mr. and Mrs. Kilbright on their wedding tour, my wife received a letter from Dr. Hildstein, written by himself from New York, but addressed in the handwriting of Mr. Corbridge.

" I return," he wrote, " to Germany, perfectly happy in having succeeded in my experiments ; but nevermore, esteemed lady, will I dematerialize a subject who has remained long enough in this world to make friends, and I am the only man who can do this thing."

This letter greatly satisfied us. " It shows that he has some heart, after all," said Mrs. Colesworthy, " but as to that man Corbridge, I believe he would have kept poor Mr. Kilbright dancing backward and forward between this world and the other as long as a dollar could be made out of him. But there is only one way in which he can do us any harm now, and that is by materializing the first Mrs. Kilbright ; but, knowing us, as he now does, I don't believe he will ever try that."

" No," said I, " I don't believe he ever will."

Should you ever meet with Mr. Amos Kilbright, you need not hesitate to entrust him with any surveying you may have on hand.   Mr. Corbridge cannot dematerialize him, the German scientist will not, and there is no one else in the world who would even think of such a thing.   Therefore, you need feel no fear that he may suddenly vanish from your sight, leaving nothing behind him but his clothes and the contents of his pockets ; unless, indeed, he should again be so foolish as to go to swim in the ocean at a point where there is a strong ebb tide.

THE REVERSIBLE LANDSCAPE.

THE REVERSIBLE LANDSCAPE.

To look at me no one would suppose it; but it is, nevertheless, a fact that I am a member of a fire company. I am somewhat middle-aged, somewhat stout, and, at certain times of the year, somewhat stiff in the joints; and my general dress and demeanor, that of a sober business man, would not at all suggest the active and impetuous fireman of the period. I do not belong to any paid department, but to a volunteer Hook and Ladder Company, composed of the active-bodied or active-minded male citizens of the country town where I live. I am included in the active-minded portion of the company; and in an organization like ours, which is not only intended to assist in putting out the fires of burning buildings, but to light the torch of the mind, this sort of member is very valuable. In the building which we occupy, our truck, with its hooks and ladders, stands upon the lower floor, while the large room above is used as a club and reading-room. At the beginning of the first winter of our occupancy of

the building, we found that this room, which had
been very pleasant in summer, was extremely uncomfortable in winter. The long apartment had
been originally intended for purposes of storage;
and although we had ornamented it and fitted it
up very neatly, a good deal of carpentry and some
mason's work was necessary before it could be
made tight and draught-proof for cold weather.
But lately we had spent money very freely, and
our treasury was absolutely empty. I was chair-
man of the committee which had charge of everything pertaining to our rooms, and I felt the re-
sponsibilities of my position. The necessary work
should be begun immediately, but how could the
money be raised to pay for it? Subscriptions for
this and that had been made until the members
were tired of that sort of thing; and the ill success of the last one showed that it would not do
to try it again.

I revolved in my mind a great many plans for
raising the sum required, and one morning, as I
was going to my place of business in the city, I
was seized with a happy idea. At the moment of
seizure I was standing in front of a large show-
window, in which were a number of oil paintings,
all of them very fresh and bright. " How would
it do," thought I to myself, " to buy a picture at a

moderate price and put it up at a raffle? People
who are not willing to give money outright will
often enter into a scheme of this kind. I will go
in and make inquiries."

When I entered I found myself in a large show-
room, the walls of which were covered with paintings. A person advanced to meet me who, as it
soon became evident, was the proprietor of the
place. He was a large man, dressed in black, with
an open shirt-front and an expansive countenance.
His eyes and hair were black, and his ears stood
out from his head in a manner which, according
to a recent writer, indicates the money-getting
faculty; and he plainly belonged to that class of
persons who in the Middle Ages did not, as is the
present custom, pay money for having their teeth
extracted, but often disbursed large sums for the
privilege of retaining them. When I asked him
if I could procure a good and effective picture at a
moderate price, he threw out his chest and waved
his arms toward his walls. " There, sir," he said,
" you can see oil paintings of every subject, of
every style, and of every class; and at prices, sir,
lower than they can be found elsewhere in the
known world. Mention the kind of picture you
want, and I can accommodate you."

I replied that I did not know exactly what I

wanted, and that I would see what he had.   I now began to look at the pictures on the walls, occasionally mentioning my ideas in regard to their merits, when suddenly my companion turned to me and said :

"Are you connected with the press, sir ? "

I replied that I was not, although I occasionally wrote for periodicals.

" Upon art subjects ? " he asked.

I answered in the negative.

" Then you are unprejudiced, " he said, " and I believe from your appearance that you are a man of influence, and there is nothing I would like better than to exhibit the workings of my art organization to a man of influence, unprejudiced on the subject.   My object is, sir, to popularize art; to place high art within the reach of the masses, and thus to educate the artistic faculties of even the poorest citizens. "

I said that I supposed the chromo movement was intended to do all that.

" No, sir, " he replied, warmly ; "chromos cannot accomplish the object.   They are too expensive ; and, besides, they are not the real thing. They are printed, not painted ; and what the public wants is the real thing, the work of the brush ; and that is what I give them.   The pictures you see here, and an immense stock besides, are all copies of valuable paintings, many of them in the finest galleries of Europe. I sell no originals. I guarantee everything to be a copy. Honesty is at the bottom of all I do. But my copies are exactly like the originals; that is all I claim. I would like, sir, to show you through my establishment, and let you see how I am carrying on the great work of art education. There are picture-dealers in this city, sir, plenty of them, who try to make the public believe that the vile daubs they sell are originals, and the works of well-known painters; and when they do admit that the picture is a copy, they say it is the work of some distinguished student; that there is no other copy in the country; or they make some other misstatement about it. These people conceal their processes, but their tricks are beginning to be well known to the public. Now, sir, I conceal nothing. The day for that sort of thing is past. I want men of influence to know the facilities I have for the production of art-work upon a grand scale. We will first go into the basement. Sir," said he, as I followed him down-stairs, "you know how the watch-making business has been revolutionized by the great companies which manufacture watches by machinery. The slow, uncertain, and expensive work of the poor toilers who made watches by hand has been superseded by the swift, unerring, and beautiful operations of machinery and steam. Now, sir, the great purpose of my life is to introduce machinery into art, and, ultimately, steam. And yet I will have no shams, no chromos. Everything shall be real—the work of the brush. Here, sir, " he continued, showing me into a long room filled with workmen, " you see the men engaged in putting together the frames on which to stretch my canvases. Every stick is cut, planed, and jointed at a mill in Vermont, and sent on here by the car-load. Beyond are the workmen cutting up, stretching, and preparing the canvas, bales upon bales of which are used in a day. At the far end are the mills for grinding and mixing colors. And now we will go to the upper floors, and see the true art-work. Here, sir, " he said, continuing to talk as we walked through the rooms on the various floors, " is the landscape and marine department. That row of men are putting in skies ; they do nothing else. Each has his copy before him, and, day after day, month after month, paints nothing but that sky ; and of course he does it with great rapidity and fidelity. Above, on those shelves, are sky-pots of every variety ; blue-serene pots, tempest pots, sunset pots in compartments, morning-gray pots, and many others. Then the work passes to the middle-ground painters, who have their half-tone pots within easy reach. After that the foreground men take it up, and the figurists put in the men and animals. That man there has been painting that foreground cow ever since the first of August. He can now put her in three and a half times in fifteen minutes, and will probably rise to sixteen cows an hour by the end of this month. These girls do nothing but put white-caps to waves. There's a great demand at present for the windy marine. This next room is devoted to portraits to order. You see that row of old ladies without heads, each holding a pair of spectacles, and with one finger in the Bible to keep the place; that's very popular, and we put in a head when the photograph is sent. There is a great rage at present for portraits of babies without any clothes on. Here is a lot of undraped infants with bodies all finished, but with no heads. We can finish them to order at very short notice. I have one girl who puts in all the dimples. You would be surprised to see what a charming dimple she can make with one twist of her brush. Long practice at one thing, sir, is the foundation of the success of this great establishment. Take that girl away from her dimple-pot, and she is nothing.

She is now upstairs, putting dimples into a large
Correggio order from the West.   This next room
is our figure department, battle-pieces, groups, single figures, everything.   As you have seen before,
each man only copies from the original that part
which is his specialty.   In addition to its other ad-
vantages, this system is a great protection to us.
None of my men can work at home at nights and
Sundays, and forge pictures.   Not one of them
can do a whole one.   And now, sir, you have seen
the greater part of my establishment.   The var-
nishing, packing, and storage rooms are in another
building.   I am now perfecting plans for the erec-
tion of an immense edifice with steam-engines in
the cellar, in which my paintings shall be done by
machinery.   No chromos, mind you, but real oil-
paintings, done by brushes revolving on cylinders.
I shall have rolls of canvas a mile long, like the
paper on which our great dailies are printed, and
the machines shall do everything ; cut off the picture, when it has passed among the cylinders,
whereupon fresh canvas will be rolled in for a new
one ; another machine will stretch them ; and they
will pass through a varnish bath in the twinkling
of an eye.   But this is in the future.   What I
want of you, sir, and of other men of influence in
society, is to let our people know of the great

good that is ready for them now, and of the greater benefit that is coming. And, more than that,
you can do incalculable good to our artists. Those
poor toilers on the solitary canvas should know
how to become prosperous, great, and happy; tell
them to go into some other business. And now,
sir, I must see what I can do for you. We will
return to my gallery, and I will show you exactly
what you want."

When we reached the back part of the show-
room, down-stairs, he brought out an unframed
picture about three feet long and two high, and
placed it in a favorable light "There," said he,
"is a picture which will suit you. It is what we
call a reversible landscape, and is copied from the
only genuine picture of the kind in the world. It
is just as good as two pictures. In this position,
you see, a line of land stretches across the middle
of the picture, with trees, houses, and figures, with
a light sky above and a lake, darker in hue, below.
Everything on the land is reflected accurately in
the water. It is a landscape in morning light.
Turn it upside down, so, and it is an evening scene;
darkening sky above, light water beneath; the
morning star, which you saw faintly glimmering
in the other picture, is now the reflection of the
evening star."

I do not pretend to be a judge of pictures, but I fancy I appreciate an original idea when I see it, and I thought that this picture might answer my purpose.

"What is the price of the painting?" I asked.

"Well, sir," said he, "to you, as a man of influence, I will fix the price of this great painting, from a comparatively unknown work of Gaspar Poussin, at four dollars and a half."

In spite of what I had seen of the facilities possessed by this establishment for producing cheap work, I must confess that I was surprised at the smallness of the sum asked for an oil-painting of that size; I had expected to give forty or fifty dollars. But, although I am not a judge of paintings, I am a business man, and accustomed to make bargains. Therefore I said:

"I will give you two dollars and fifty cents for the picture."

"Done," said he. "Where shall I send it?"

I gave him my city address, and paid the money. As he accompanied me to the door, he said: "If you would like more of these pictures, I will sell you one dozen for eighteen dollars, or the whole lot of one hundred, just finished—and there will be no more of them painted—for one hundred dollars." I told him one was all I wanted, and departed. I carried the picture home that afternoon, and in the evening exhibited it at our club-room, and made known my scheme for raising the money we needed by getting up a raffle with this painting as the prize ; one hundred tickets at the low price of two dollars each. The reversible land-scape was set up, first one way and then the other, a great many times, and created quite a sensation.

" I don't think it's worth the half of two hundred dollars," said Mr. Buckby, our president, "but as the money is for the use of our Association, I don't mind that. But my objection to the scheme is that, if I should gain the prize, I should be laughed at by all my fellow-members : for, to tell the truth, I think that painting is a good deal more funny than otherwise. It's not what I call high art."

The other members generally agreed with him. They were very much amused by the picture, but they did not care to possess it, imagining that those who ridiculed it might also ridicule its owner. This opposition discouraged me, and I retired to reflect. In about five minutes I returned to the company, which had now greatly increased, as it was one of our regular meeting nights, and I asked if they would consent to this raffle if I would

engage that the winner of the picture should not
be laughed at by any other member.

"How will you guarantee that?" asked Mr.
Buckby.

"I will put the matter in the hands of the Association," I answered.   "If, after the raffle is over,
a majority of the members shall decide that any
of us have reason to laugh at the winner of this
painting, I will refund all the money paid for
tickets."

There was something in this proposition which
aroused the curiosity of my fellow-firemen; and
when the meeting was called to order, a resolution
was adopted that we would have the raffle, and
that the management of it should be placed in my
hands, subject to the conditions mentioned above.
There were a good many surmises as to what I
was going to do to keep the people from laughing
at the prize-winner, the general opinion being that
I intended to have the picture altered so that it
would be like an ordinary landscape, and not reversible.   But the affair was something novel, and
promised to put the much-needed money into our
treasury; and several gentlemen assured me that
they would make it their business to see that
every member took a ticket, one generous man
promising, in the interests of the Association, to

present them to such of the few members as might decline to buy them for themselves. This offer was made in consequence of my insistance that every one of us should have a chance in the raffle.

The next morning I went to the art-factory and told the proprietor that I would take the lot of reversibles he had on hand, if he would include the one already purchased, and receive ninety-seven dollars and a half as the balance due.

" All right !" said he. " I have the ninety-nine still on hand. Are you in the tea business, sir ? "

" Oh, no," said I ; "the pictures are intended for a large Association."

" No better way of extending the influence of art, sir," he said, heartily. " I shall charge you nothing for boxing. The same address, sir ? "

" No, they must be forwarded to my residence," and I gave him the needful directions, and a check.

The next day the ninety-nine pictures arrived and were stored in my barn. My wife, to whom I had told my plan, made some objections to it, saying it did not seem right to use half the money paid in to buy so many pictures; but I told her that no one could expect in a raffle to clear all the money subscribed, and that although we should not gain as much as I had hoped, we should clear a hundred dollars, and every man would have a picture. This was surely fair, and the fact was that the unsympathetic state of mind of our members made it necessary for me to do something of this kind, if I expected to raise the needed money at all.

The raffle was announced, and on the appointed evening there was a full attendance. The prize was won by a Mr. Horter, an art-collector of a nervous temperament, who had objected to the raffle, and who had consented to buy a ticket only after repeated solicitations.

"Now mind," he said to me, "you promised that the other men should not laugh at me, and I hold you to your contract."

I answered that I intended to stand by it, and that the painting should be sent to him in the morning from my house, whither it had been removed. Every member present announced his intention of calling on Horter the following evening to see why he should not be laughed at.

All the next forenoon my man, with a horse and light wagon, was engaged in delivering the reversible landscapes, one to every member of our club. These gentlemen were, in almost every case, absent at their places of business. When they came home in the evening each found his picture, with his name on the back of it, and a printed slip informing him that in this raffle there had been no blanks, and that every man had drawn a prize.

Not a man called upon Mr. Horter that evening, and he greatly wondered why they did not come in, either to laugh or to say why they should not do so; but every other member of our club was visited by nearly all his fellow-firemen, who ran in to see if it were true that he also had one of those ridiculous reversible landscapes. As everybody knew that Mr. Horter had one, there was no need to call on him; and even if they had hoped to be able to laugh at him they could not do so, when each of them had drawn one of the pictures himself. A good many called on me, and some were a little severe in their remarks, saying that although it might be a very pretty joke, I must have used up nearly all the money that they had given for the good of the Association, for, of course, none of them cared for the absurd prize.

But when, on the next meeting night, I paid in one hundred dollars to the treasury, a sum more than sufficient to make our room comfortable, they were quite satisfied. The only thing that troubled them was to know what to do with the pictures

6

they had drawn. Not one of them was willing to keep his preposterous landscape in his house. It was Mrs. Buckby, our president's wife, who suggested a way out of the difficulty.

"Of course," she said to her husband, "it would have been much better if each one of you had given the two dollars without any raffle, and then you would have had all your money. But one can't expect men to do a thing like that."

"Not after we had all paid in our regular dues, and had been subscribing and subscribing for this, that, and the other thing for nearly a year," said I, who was present at the time. "Some extra inducement was necessary."

"But, as you have all those horrid landscapes," she continued, "why don't you take them and put them up along the top of your walls, next the ceiling, where those openings are which used to ventilate the room when it was used for storage? That would save all the money that you would have to pay to carpenters and painters to have those places made tight and decent-looking; and it would give your room a gorgeous appearance."

This idea was hailed with delight. Every man brought his picture to the hall, and we nailed the whole hundred in a row along the top of the four walls, turning one with the darker half up, and

the next the other way, so as to present alternate
views of morning and evening along the whole
distance. The arrangement answered admirably.
The draughts of air from outside were perfectly
excluded : and as our walls were very lofty, the
general effect was good.

"Art of that kind cannot be too high," said Mr.
Horter.

A week or two after this, when I arrived at
home one afternoon, my wife told me that there
was a present for me in the dining-room. As such
things were not common, I hurried in to see what
it was. I found a very large flat package, tied up
in brown paper, and on it a card with my name
and a long inscription. The latter was to the
effect that my associates of the Hook and Ladder
Company, desirous of testifying their gratitude to
the originator and promoter of the raffle scheme,
took pleasure in presenting him with the accompa-
nying work of art, which, when hung upon the
walls of his house, would be a perpetual reminder
to him of the great and good work he had done
for the Association.

I cannot deny that this pleased me much.

"Well!" I exclaimed to my wife, "it is very
seldom that a man gets any thanks for his gratui-

tous efforts in behalf of his fellow-beings; and although I must say that my services in raising money for the Association deserved recognition, I did not expect that the members would do themselves the justice to make me a present."

Unwrapping the package, I discovered, to my intense disgust, a copy of the Reversible Landscape! My first thought was that some of the members, for a joke, had taken down one of the paintings from our meeting-room and had sent it to me; but, on carefully examining the canvas and frame, I was quite certain that this picture had never been nailed to a wall. It was evidently a new and fresh copy of the painting of which I had been assured no more would be produced. I must admit that I had felt a certain pride in decorating our hall with the style of picture that could not be seen elsewhere; and, moreover, I greatly dislike to be overreached in business matters, and my wrath against the manufacturer of high art entirely overpowered and dissipated any little resentment I might have felt against my waggish fellow-members who had sent me the painting.

Early the next morning I went direct to the art-factory, and was just about entering when my attention was attracted by a prominent picture in the window. I stepped back to look at it. It was our reversible landscape, mounted upon an easel, and labelled " A Morning Scene." While I examined it to assure myself that it was really the landscape with which I was so familiar, it was turned upside down by some concealed machinery, and appeared labelled, " An Evening Scene." At the foot of the easel I now noticed a placard inscribed: " The Reversible Landscape: A New Idea in Art."

I stood for a moment astounded. The rascally picture-monger had not only made another of these pictures, but he was prepared to furnish them in any number. Rushing into the gallery, I demanded to see the proprietor.

"Look here!" said I, "what does this mean? You told me that there were to be no more of those pictures painted; that I was to possess a unique lot."

" That's not the same picture, sir," he exclaimed. " I am surprised that you should think so. Step outside with me, sir, and I'll prove it to you. There, sir!" said he, as we stood before the painting, which was now Morning side up, "you see that star? In the pictures we sold you the morning star was Venus; in this one it is Jupiter. This is not the same picture. Do you imagine that we would deceive a customer? That, sir, is a thing we never do!"

DUSKY PHILOSOPHY.

.

DUSKY PHILOSOPHY.

IN TWO EXPOSITIONS.

FIRST EXPOSITION: A STORY OF SEVEN DEVILS.

The negro church which stood in the pine-woods near the little village of Oxford Cross Roads, in one of the lower counties of Virginia, was presided over by an elderly individual, known to the community in general as Uncle Pete; but on Sundays the members of his congregation addressed him as Brudder Pete. He was an earnest and energetic man, and, although he could neither read nor write, he had for many years expounded the Scriptures to the satisfaction of his hearers. His memory was good, and those portions of the Bible, which from time to time he had heard read, were used by him, and frequently with powerful effect, in his sermons. His interpretations of the Scriptures were generally entirely original, and were made to suit the needs, or what he supposed to be the needs, of his congregation.

Whether as "Uncle Pete" in the garden and corn-field, or "Brudder Pete" in the church, he enjoyed the good opinion of everybody excepting one person, and that was his wife. She was a high-tempered and somewhat dissatisfied person, who had conceived the idea that her husband was in the habit of giving too much time to the church, and too little to the acquisition of corn-bread and pork. On a certain Saturday she gave him a most tremendous scolding, which so affected the spirits of the good man that it influenced his decision in regard to the selection of the subject for his sermon the next day.

His congregation was accustomed to being astonished, and rather liked it, but never before had their minds received such a shock as when the preacher announced the subject of his discourse. He did not take any particular text, for this was not his custom, but he boldly stated that the Bible declared that every woman in this world was possessed by seven devils; and the evils which this state of things had brought upon the world he showed forth with much warmth and feeling. Subject-matter, principally from his own experience, crowded in upon his mind, and he served it out to his audience hot and strong. If his deductions could have been proved to be correct, all women were creatures who, by reason of their seven-fold diabolic possession, were not capable of independent thought or action, and who should in tears and humility place themselves absolutely under the direction and authority of the other sex.

When he approached the conclusion of his sermon, Brother Peter closed with a bang the Bible, which, although he could not read a word of it, always lay open before him while he preached, and delivered the concluding exhortation of his sermon.

"Now, my dear brev'ren ob dis congregation," he said, " I want you to understan' dat dar's nuffin in dis yer sarmon wot you've jus' heerd ter make you think yousefs angels. By no means, brev'ren ; you was all brung up by women, an' you've got ter lib wid' em, an ef anythin' in dis yer worl' is ketchin', my dear brev'ren, it's habin debbils, an' from wot I've seen ob some ob de men ob dis worl' I 'spect dey is persest ob 'bout all de debbils dey got room fur. But de Bible don' say nuffin p'intedly on de subjec' ob de number ob debbils in man, an' I 'spec' dose dat's got 'em—an' we ought ter feel pow'ful thankful, my dear brev'ren, dat de Bible don' say we all's got 'em—has 'em 'cordin to sarcumstances. But wid de women it's dif'rent ; dey's got jus' sebin, an' bless my soul, brev'ren, I think dat's 'nuff.

"While I was a-turnin' ober in my min' de subjec' ob dis sarmon, dere come ter me a bit ob
Scripter wot I heerd at a big preachin' an' baptizin'
at Kyarter's Mills, 'bout ten year' ago. One ob de
preachers was a-tellin' about ole mudder Ebe
a-eatin' de apple, and says he : De sarpint fus'
come along wid a red apple, an' says he : You gib
dis yer to your husban', an' he think it so
mighty good dat when he done eat it he gib you
anything you ax him fur, ef you tell him whar
de tree is. Ebe, she took one bite, an' den she
frew dat apple away. ' Wot you mean, you triflin'
sarpint,' says she, 'a fotchin' me dat apple wot ain't
good fur nuffin but ter make cider wid.' Den de
sarpint he go fotch her a yaller apple, an' she took
one bite an' den says she : ' Go 'long wid ye, you
fool sarpint, wot you fotch me dat June apple wot
ain't got no taste to it ?' Den de sarpint he think
she like sumpin' sharp, an' he fotch her a green
apple. She takes one bite ob it, an' den she frows
it at his head, an' sings out : ' Is you 'spectin' me to
gib dat apple to yer Uncle Adam an' gib him de
colic ?' Den de debbil he fotch her a lady-apple,
but she say she won't take no sich triflin' nubbins
as dat to her husban', an' she took one bite ob it,
an' frew it away. Den he go fotch her two udder
kin' ob apples, one yaller wid red stripes, an' de

udder one red on one side an' green on de udder, —mighty good lookin' apples, too—de kin' you git two dollars a bar'l fur at the store. But Ebe, she wouldn't hab neider ob 'em, an' when she done took one bite out ob each one, she frew it away. Den de ole debbil-sarpint, he scratch he head, an' he say to hese'f: 'Dis yer Ebe, she pow'ful 'ticklar 'bout her apples. Reckin I'll have ter wait till after fros', an' fotch her a real good one.' An' he done wait till after fros', and then he fotch her a' Albemarle pippin, an' when she took one bite ob dat, she jus' go 'long an' eat it all up, core, seeds, an' all. 'Look h'yar, sarpint,' says she, 'hab you got anudder ob dem apples in your pocket?' An' den he tuk one out, an' gib it to her. ''Cuse me,' says she, 'I's gwine ter look up Adam, an' ef he don' want ter know war de tree is wot dese apples grow on, you can hab him fur a corn-field han'.'

"An' now, my dear brev'ren," said Brother Peter, "while I was a-turnin' dis subjec' ober in my min', an' wonderin' how de women come ter hab jus' seben debbils apiece, I done reckerleck dat bit ob Scripter wot I heerd at Kyarter's Mills, an' I reckin dat 'splains how de debbils got inter woman. De sarpint he done fotch mudder Ebe seben apples, an' ebery one she take a bite out of gib her a debbil."

As might have been expected, this sermon produced a great sensation, and made a deep impres-
sion on the congregation. As a rule the men were
tolerably well satisfied with it; and when the
services were over many of them made it the occasion of shy but very plainly pointed remarks to
their female friends and relatives.

But the women did not like it at all. Some of
them became angry, and talked very forcibly, and
feelings of indignation soon spread among all the
sisters of the church. If their minister had seen fit
to stay at home and preach a sermon like this to
his own wife (who, it may be remarked, was not
present on this occasion), it would have been well
enough, provided he had made no allusions to
outsiders; but to come there and preach such
things to them was entirely too much for their
endurance. Each one of the women knew she had
not seven devils, and only a few of them would
admit of the possibility of any of the others being
possessed by quite so many.

Their preacher's explanation of the manner in
which every woman came to be possessed of just
so many devils appeared to them of little impor-
tance. What they objected to was the fundamental
doctrine of his sermon, which was based on his
assertion that the Bible declared every woman had

seven devils. They were not willing to believe that the Bible said any such thing. Some of them went so far as to state it was their opinion that Uncle Pete had got this fool notion from some of the lawyers at the court-house when he was on a jury a month or so before. It was quite noticeable that, although Sunday afternoon had scarcely begun, the majority of the women of the congregation called their minister Uncle Pete. This was very strong evidence of a sudden decline in his popularity.

Some of the more vigorous-minded women, not seeing their minister among the other people in the clearing in front of the log church, went to look for him, but he was not to be found. His wife had ordered him to be home early, and soon after the congregation had been dismissed he departed by a short cut through the woods. That afternoon an irate committee, composed principally of women, but including also a few men who had expressed disbelief in the new doctrine, arrived at the cabin of their preacher, but found there only his wife, cross-grained old Aunt Rebecca. She informed them that her husband was not at home.

"He's done 'gaged hisse'f," she said, "ter cut an' haul wood fur Kunnel Martin ober on Little Mount'n fur de whole ob nex' week. It's fourteen or thirteen mile' from h'yar, an' ef he'd started ter-morrer mawnin', he'd los' a'mos' a whole day. 'Sides dat, I done tole him dat ef he git dar ter-night he'd have his supper frowed in. Wot you all want wid him? Gwine to pay him fur preachin'?"

Any such intention as this was instantaneously denied, and Aunt Rebecca was informed of the subject upon which her visitors had come to have a very plain talk with her husband.

Strange to say, the announcement of the new and startling dogma had apparently no disturbing effect upon Aunt Rebecca. On the contrary, the old woman seemed rather to enjoy the news.

"Reckin he oughter know all 'bout dat," she said. "He's done had three wives, an' he ain't got rid o' dis one yit."

Judging from her chuckles and waggings of the head when she made this remark, it might be imagined that Aunt Rebecca was rather proud of the fact that her husband thought her capable of exhibiting a different kind of diabolism every day in the week.

The leader of the indignant church members was Susan Henry, a mulatto woman of a very independent turn of mind. She prided herself that she never worked in anybody's house but her own, and this immunity from outside service gave her a certain pre-eminence among her sisters. Not only did Susan share the general resentment with which the startling statement of old Peter had been received, but she felt that its promulgation had affected her position in the community. If every woman was possessed by seven devils, then, in this respect, she was no better nor worse than any of the others; and at this her proud heart rebelled. If the preacher had said some women had eight devils and others six, it would have been better. She might then have made a mental arrangement in regard to her relative position which would have somewhat consoled her. But now there was no chance for that. The words of the preacher had equally debased all women.

A meeting of the disaffected church members was held the next night at Susan Henry's cabin, or rather in the little yard about it, for the house was not large enough to hold the people who attended it. The meeting was not regularly organized, but everybody said what he or she had to say, and the result was a great deal of clamor, and a general increase of indignation against Uncle Pete.

" Look h'yar!" cried Susan, at the end of some energetic remarks, " is dar enny pusson h'yar who kin count up figgers ?"

7

Inquiries on the subject ran through the crowd, and in a few moments a black boy, about fourteen, was pushed forward as an expert in arithmetic.

"Now, you Jim," said Susan, "you's been to school, an' you kin count up figgers. 'Cordin' ter de chu'ch books dar's forty-seben women b'longin' to our meetin', an' ef each one ob dem dar has got seben debbils in her, I jus' wants you ter tell me how many debbils come to chu'ch ebery clear Sunday ter hear dat ole Uncle Pete preach."

This view of the case created a sensation, and much interest was shown in the result of Jim's calculations, which were made by the aid of a back of an old letter and a piece of pencil furnished by Susan. The result was at last announced as three hundred and nineteen, which, although not precisely correct, was near enough to satisfy the company.

"Now, you jus' turn dat ober in you all's minds," said Susan. "More'n free hunderd debbils in chu'ch ebery Sunday, an' we women fotchin 'em. Does anybody s'pose I'se gwine ter b'lieve dat fool talk?"

A middle-aged man now lifted up his voice and said: "Ise been thinkin' ober dis h'yar matter and Ise 'cluded dat p'r'aps de words ob de preacher was used in a figgeratous form o' sense. P'r'aps de seben debbils meant chillun."

These remarks were received with no favor by the assemblage.

" Oh, you git out !" cried Susan. " Your ole woman's got seben chillun, shore 'nuf, an' I s'pec' dey's all debbils. But dem sent'ments don't apply ter all de udder women h'yar, 'tic'larly ter dem dar young uns wot ain't married yit."

This was good logic, but the feeling on the subject proved to be even stronger, for the mothers in the company became so angry at their children being considered devils that for a time there seemed to be danger of an Amazonian attack on the unfortunate speaker. This was averted, but a great deal of uproar now ensued, and it was the general feeling that something ought to be done to show the deep-seated resentment with which the horrible charge against the mothers and sisters of the congregation had been met. Many violent propositions were made, some of the younger men going so far as to offer to burn down the church. It was finally agreed, quite unanimously, that old Peter should be unceremoniously ousted from his place in the pulpit which he had filled so many years.

As the week passed on, some of the older men of the congregation who had friendly feelings toward their old companion and preacher talked the matter over among themselves, and afterward, with many of their fellow-members, succeeded at last in gaining the general consent that Uncle Pete should be allowed a chance to explain himself, and give his grounds and reasons for his astounding statement in regard to womankind. If he could show biblical authority for this, of course nothing more could be said. But if he could not, then he must get down from the pulpit, and sit for the rest of his life on a back seat of the church. This proposition met with the more favor, because even those who were most indignant had an earnest curiosity to know what the old man would say for himself.

During all this time of angry discussion, good old Peter was quietly and calmly cutting and hauling wood on the Little Mountain. His mind was in a condition of great comfort and peace, for not only had he been able to rid himself, in his last sermon, of many of the hard thoughts concerning women that had been gathering themselves together for years, but his absence from home had given him a holiday from the harassments of Aunt Rebecca's tongue, so that no new notions of woman's culpability had risen within him. He had dismissed the subject altogether, and had been thinking over a sermon regarding baptism, which he thought he could make convincing to certain of the younger members of his congregation.

He arrived at home very late on Saturday night, and retired to his simple couch without knowing anything of the terrible storm which had been gathering through the week, and which was to burst upon him on the morrow. But the next morning, long before church time, he received warning enough of what was going to happen. Individuals and deputations gathered in and about his cabin—some to tell him all that had been said and done; some to inform him what was expected of him; some to stand about and look at him; some to scold; some to denounce; but, alas! not one to encourage; nor one to call him " Brudder Pete," that Sunday appellation dear to his ears. But the old man possessed a stubborn soul, not easily to be frightened.

" Wot I says in de pulpit," he remarked, " I'll 'splain in de pulpit, an' you all ud better git 'long to de chu'ch, an' when de time fur de sarvice come, I'll be dar."

This advice was not promptly acted upon, but in the course of half an hour nearly all the villagers and loungers had gone off to the church in the woods; and when Uncle Peter had put on his high black hat, somewhat battered, but still sufficiently clerical looking for that congregation, and had given something of a polish to his cowhide

shoes, he betook himself by the accustomed path
to the log building where he had so often held
forth to his people. As soon as he entered the
church he was formally instructed by a committee
of the leading members that before he began to
open the services, he must make it plain to the
congregation that what he had said on the preced-
ing Sunday about every woman being possessed by
seven devils was Scripture truth, and not mere
wicked nonsense out of his own brain. If he could
not do that, they wanted no more praying or
preaching from him.

Uncle Peter made no answer, but, ascending the
little pulpit, he put his hat on the bench behind
him where it was used to repose, took out his red
cotton handkerchief and blew his nose in his accustomed way, and looked about him. The house
was crowded. Even Aunt Rebecca was there.

After a deliberate survey of his audience the
preacher spoke : " Brev'eren an' sisters, I see afore
me Brudder Bill Hines, who kin read de Bible, an'
has got one. Ain't dat so, Brudder?"

Bill Hines having nodded and modestly grunt-
ed assent, the preacher continued. "An' dars'
Aun' Priscilla's boy, Jake, who ain't a brudder
yit, though he's plenty old 'nuf, min,' I tell ye ;
an' he kin read de Bible, fus' rate, an' has read

it ter me ober an' ober ag'in. Ain't dat so, Jake?"

Jake grinned, nodded, and hung his head, very uncomfortable at being thus publicly pointed out.

"An' dar's good ole Aun' Patty, who knows more Scripter' dan ennybuddy h'yar, havin' been teached by de little gals from Kunnel Jasper's an' by dere mudders afore 'em. I reckin she know' de hull Bible straight froo, from de Garden of Eden to de New Jerus'lum. An' dar are udders h'yar who knows de Scripters, some one part an' some anudder. Now I axes ebery one ob you all wot know de Scripters ef he don' 'member how de Bible tells how our Lor' when he was on dis yearth cas' seben debbils out o' Mary Magdalum?"

A murmur of assent came from the congregation. Most of them remembered that.

"But did enny ob you ebber read, or hab read to you, dat he ebber cas' 'em out o' enny udder woman?"

Negative grunts and shakes of the head signified that nobody had ever heard of this.

"Well, den," said the preacher, gazing blandly around, "all de udder women got 'em yit."

A deep silence fell upon the assembly, and in a few moments an elderly member arose. "Brudder Pete," he said, "I reckin you mought as well gib out de hyme."

SECOND EXPOSITION : GRANDISON'S QUANDARY.

Grandison Pratt was a colored man of about thirty, who, with his wife and two or three children, lived in a neat log cabin in one of the Southern States. He was a man of an independent turn of mind, and he much desired to own the house in which he lived and the small garden-patch around it. This valuable piece of property belonged to Mr. Morris, and as it was an outlying corner of his large farm he had no objection to sell it to Grandison, provided the latter could pay for it; but of this he had great doubts. The man was industrious enough, but he often seemed to have a great deal of difficulty about paying the very small rental charged for his place, and Mr. Morris, consequently, had well-grounded doubts about his ability to purchase it.

" But, sah," said Grandison one day when these objections had been placed before him, " I's been turnin' dis thing ober in my min' ober an' ober. I know jes' how much I kin make an' how much I's got to spend an' how I kin save ter buy the house, an' if I agree to pay you so much money on such a day an' so much on such anudder day I's gwine ter do it. You kin jes' put that down, sah, for sartin shuh."

"Well, Grandison," said Mr. Morris, " I'll give you a trial. If, at the end of six months, you can pay me the first instalment, I'll have the necessary papers made out, and you can go on and buy the place, but if you are not up to time on the first payment, I want to hear no more about the purchase."

" All right, Mahs'r Morris," said Grandison. " If I gibs you my word ter pay de money on de fus' day ob October, I's gwine to do it. Dat's sartin shuh."

Months passed on, and, although Grandison worked as steadily as usual, he found toward the end of September that, in the ordinary course of things, he would not be able to make up the sum necessary for the first payment. Other methods out of the ordinary course came into his mind, but he had doubts about availing himself of them. He was extremely anxious to make up the amount due, for he knew very well that if he did not pay it on the day appointed he might bid farewell to his hope of becoming a freeholder. In his perplexity he resolved to consult Brother 'Bijah, the minister of the little church in the pine-woods to which Grandison belonged.

" Now, look-a-heah, Brudder 'Bijah," said he, " wot's I gwine to do 'bout dis bizness? I done promised ter pay dis money on de fus' day ob de comin' month, an' dar's six dollars ob it dat I ain't got yit."

"An' aint dar any way ter git it?" asked 'Bijah.

"Yaas, dar's one way," said Grandison. "I's been turnin' dis matter ober an' ober in my min', an' dar's only one way. I mought sell apples. Apples is mighty skarse dis fall, an' I kin git two dollars a bar'l for 'em in town. Now, if I was ter sell three bar'ls of apples I'd hab dat dar six dollars, sartin shuh. Don' you see dat, Brudder 'Bijah?"

"Dat's all clar 'nuf," said the minister, "but whar you gwine ter git three bar'ls o' apples? You don' mean ter tell me dat you's got 'nuf apple-trees in your little gyardin fur ter shake down three bar'ls o' apples."

"Now look a-heah, Brudder 'Bijah," said Grandison, his eyes sparkling with righteous indignation, "dat's too much to 'spec' ob a man who's got ter work all day to s'port his wife an' chillun. I digs, an' I plows, an' I plants, an' I hoes. But all dem things ain't 'nuf ter make apple-trees grow in my gyardin like as dey was corn-field peas."

"Dat's so," said 'Bijah, reflectively. "Dat's too much to spec' ob any man. But how's you gwine ter sell de apples if you ain't got 'em?"

"I's got ter git em," said Grandison. "Dar's

apples 'nuf growin' roun' an' not so fur away dat I can't tote 'em ter my house in a bahsket. It's pow'ful hard on a man wot's worked all day ter have ter tote apples ahfter night, but dar ain' no other way ob gittin' dat dar money."

"I spec' de orchard whar you's thinkin' o' gwine is Mahs'r Morrises," said the minister.

"You don' 'spose Ise gwine ter any ob dose low down orchards on de udder side de creek, does ye? Mahs'r Morris has got the bes' apples in dis county. Dat's de kin' wot fetch two dollars a bar'l."

"Brudder Gran'son," said 'Bijah, solemnly, "is you min' runnin on takin' Mahs'r Morrises apples inter town an' sellin' em?"

"Well, he gits de money, don't he?" answered the other, "and if I don't sell his apples 'taint no use sellin' none. Dem udder little nubbins roun' heah won't fetch no two dollars a bar'l."

"Dem ain't justifyin' deeds wot's runnin' in your mind," said 'Bijah. "Dey ain't justifyin'."

"Ob course," said Grandison, "dey wouldn't be justifyin' if I had de six dollars. But I ain't got 'em, an' Ise promised to pay 'em. Now, is I ter stick to de truf, or isn't I?"

"Truf is mighty," said the preacher, "an' ought not to be hendered from prevailin'."

"Dat's so! dat's so!" exclaimed Grandison.

" You can't go agin de Scripters.   Truf *is* mighty,
an' 'tain't fur pore human critters like us to try to
upsot her.   Wot we're got ter do is ter stick to her
through thick an' thin."

" Ob course, dat's wot we oughter do," said 'Bijah, "but I can't see my way clar to you sellin' dem
apples."

" But dar ain't nuffin else ter do!" exclaimed
Grandison, "an' ef I don't do dat, away goes de
truf, clar out o' sight.   An' wot sort o' 'ligion you
call dat, Brudder 'Bijah ? "

" 'Tain't no kind at all," said 'Bijah, " fur we's
bound ter stick to de truf, which is de bottom
corner-stone ob piousness.   But dem apples don't
seem ter git demselves straightened out in my
mind, Brudder Gran'son."

" It 'pears ter me, Brudder 'Bijah, dat you doan'
look at dem apples in de right light.   If I was
gwine ter sell 'em to git money ter buy a lot o'
spotted calliker ter make frocks for de chillen, or
eben to buy two pars o' shoes fur me an' Judy ter
go to church in, dat would be a sin, sartin shuh.
But you done furgit dat I's gwine ter take de
money ter Mahs'r Morris.   If apples is riz an' I
gits two dollars an' a quarter a bar'l, ob course I
keeps de extry quarter, which don' pay anyhow
fur de trouble ob pickin' 'em.   But de six dollars I

gibs, cash down, ter Mahs'r Morris. Don' you
call dat puffectly fa'r an' squar, Brudder 'Bijah ? "

'Bijah shook his head. "Dis is a mighty dubersome question, Brudder Gran'son, a mighty dubersome question."

Grandison stood with a disappointed expression
on his countenance. He greatly desired to gain
from his minister sanction for the financial opera-
tion he had proposed. But this the solemn 'Bijah
did not appear prepared to give. As the two men
stood together by the roadside they saw, riding
toward them, Mr. Morris himself.

" Now, den," exclaimed Grandison, " heah comes
Mahs'r Morris, and I's gwine ter put dis question
to hisse'f. He oughter know how ter 'cide bout
it, if anybody does."

"You ain't truly gwine ter put dat question to
him, is ye ? " asked 'Bijah, quickly.

"No, sah," replied the other. " I's gwine to
put the case on a dif'rent show-pint. But 'twill
be the same thing as de udder."

Mr. Morris was a genial-natured man, who took
a good deal of interest in his negro neighbors, and
was fond of listening to their peculiar humor.
Therefore, when he saw that Grandison wished to
speak to him he readily pulled up his horse.

" Mahs'r Morris," said Grandison, removing his

hat, " Brudder 'Bijah an' me has been argyin on de subjick ob truf. An' jes' as you was comin' up I was gwine ter tell him a par'ble 'bout sticken ter truf. An' if you's got time, Mahs'r Morris, I'd be pow'ful glad ter tell you de par'ble, an' let you 'cide 'tween us."

" Very well," said Mr. Morris, " go on with your parable."

" Dis yere par'ble," said Grandison, " has got a justifyin' meanin' in it, an' it's 'bout a bar an' a' possum. De 'possum he was a-gwine out early in de mawnin' ter git a little corn fur his breakfus'——"

" Very wrong in the opossum," said Mr. Morris, " for I am sure he hadn't planted any corn."

" Well, den, sah," said Grandison, " p'raps 'twas akerns; but, anyway, afore he was out ob de woods he see a big, ole bar a-comin' straight 'long to him. De 'possum he ain't got no time ter climb a tree an' git out on de leetlest end ob a long limb, an' so he lay hese'f flat down on de groun' an' make b'lieve he's dead. When de ole bar came up he sot down an' look at de 'possum. Fus' he turn his head on one side an' den he turn his head on de udder, but he look at de 'possum all de time. D'reckly he gits done lookin' an' he says :

" ' Look-a-heah, 'possum, is you dead or is you libin'? If you's dead I won't eat you, fur I neber

eats dead critters, but if you's libin' den I eats you
for my breakfus,' fur I is bilin' hungry, not havin'
had nuffin sence sun-up but a little smack dat I
took afore gwine out inter de damp air ob de
mawnin'. Now, den, 'possum, speak out and tell
me is you 'libe or is you dead ? '

"Dat are question frew de 'possum inter a pow'-
ful sweat. If he told de truf an' said he was alibe
he knowed well 'nuf dat de bar would gobble him
up quicker'n if he'd been a hot ash cake an' a bowl
of buttermilk ; but if he said he was dead so's de
bar wouldn't eat him, de bar, like 'nuf, would know
he lied, an' would eat him all de same. So he
turn de matter ober an' ober in his min', an' he
wrastled with his 'victions, but he couldn't come
ter no 'clusion. 'Now don't you tink,' said de
bar, 'dat I's got time to sit here de whole mawnin' waitin' fer you ter make up your mind whether
you's dead or not. If you don't 'cide pretty quick,
I'll put a big rock a-top o' you, an' stop fer you
answer when I come back in de ebenin'.' Now
dis gib de 'possum a pow'ful skeer, an' 'twas cl'ar
to his min' dat he mus' 'cide de question straight
off. If he tole de truf, and said he was alibe, he'd
be eat up shuh ; but if he said he was dead, de
bar mought b'lieve him. 'Twarn't very likely dat
he would, but dar was dat one leetle chance, an'

he done took it. 'I is dead,' says he. 'You's
a long time makin' up your min' 'bout it,' says
de bar. 'How long you been dead?' 'Sence
day 'fore yestidday,' says the 'possum. 'All
right!' says de bar, 'when dey've on'y been dead
two or free days, an' kin talk, I eats 'em all de
same.' An' he eat him up."

"And now, Grandison," said Mr. Morris,
"where is the moral of that parable?"

"De moral is dis," said Grandison; "stick ter
de truf. If de 'possum had tole de truf, an' said he
was alibe, de bar couldn't eat him no more'n he
did eat him; no bar could do dat. An' I axes you,
Mahs'r Morris, don' dat par'ble show dat eb'rybody
oughter stick ter de truf, no matter what happens."

"Well, I don't think your moral is very clear,"
said Mr. Morris, "for it would have been about as
bad for the 'possum one way as the other. But, after
all, it would have been better for the little beast to
tell the truth and die with a clear conscience."

"Dat's so!" cried Brother 'Bijah, speaking in
his ministerial capacity, "de great thing in dis
worl' is ter die wid a clear conscience."

"But you can't do dat," said Grandison, "if you
let dis thing an' dat thing come in ter hinder ye.
Now dat's jes' wot we's been disputin' 'bout, Mahs'r
Morris. I 'clared dat we oughter stick ter de truf

widout lookin' to de right or de lef'; but Brudder 'Bijah, his min' wasn't quite made up on de subjick. Now, wot you say, Mahs'r Morris?"

"I say stick to the truth, of course," said Mr. Morris, gathering up his reins. "And, by the way, Grandison, do you expect to make that payment on your place which is due next week ?"

"Yaas, sah, sartin shuh," said Grandison. "I done tole you I'd do it, Mahs'r Morris, an' I 'tends ter stick ter de truf."

"Now, den," said Grandison, in a tone of triumph, when Mr. Morris had ridden away, "you see I's right in my 'clusions, and Mahs'r Morris 'grees with me."

"Dunno," said Brother 'Bijah, shaking his head, "dis is a mighty dubersome question. You kep' dem apples clar out o' sight, Brudder Gran'son; clar out o' sight."

It was about a week after this, quite early in the morning, that Grandison was slowly driving into town with a horse and a wagon which he had borrowed from a neighbor. In the wagon were three barrels of fine apples. Suddenly, at a turn in the road, he was greatly surprised to meet Mr. Morris, riding homeward.

"What have you in those barrels, Grandison?" inquired his landlord.

8

"Dey's apples, sah," was the reply, "dat I's got de job ob haulin' ter town, sah."

Mr. Morris rode up to the wagon and removed the piece of old canvas that was thrown over the tops of the barrels; there was no need of asking any questions. No one but himself, for many miles around, had "Belle-flowers" and "Jeannettes" like these.

"How much do you lack, Grandison," he said, "of making up the money you owe me to-morrow?"

"Six dollars, sah," said Grandison.

"Six dollars—three barrels—very good," said Mr. Morris. "I see you are determined to stick to the truth, Grandison, and keep your engagement. But I will trouble you to turn that wagon round and haul those apples to my house. And, if you still want to buy the place, you can come on Monday morning and work out the balance you have to make up on the first instalment; and, after this, you can make all your payments in work. A day's labor is fair and plain, but your ways of sticking to the truth are very crooked."

It was not long after this that Grandison was ploughing in one of Mr. Morris' fields, when Brother 'Bijah came along and sat upon the fence.

"Brudder Gran'son," said he, when the ploughman had reached the end of the furrow and was preparing to turn, " jes' you let your hoss res' a minnit till I tells you a par'ble."

" Wot par'ble ?" said Grandison, in a tone of unconcern, but stopping his horse, all the same.

" Why, dis one!" said 'Bijah. " Dar was an ole mule an' he b'longed to a cullud man named Harris who used to carry de mail from de Coht House ter Cary's Cross-roads. De ole mule was a pow'ful triflin' critter an' he got lazier an' lazier, an' 'fore long he got so dreffle slow dat it tuk him more'n one day ter go from de Coht House ter de cross-roads, an' he allus come in de day ahfter mail-day, when de people was done gone home. So de cullud man, Harris, he says :

" 'You is too ole fur ter carry de mail, you triflin' mule, an' I hain't got no udder use fur you.'

" So he put him in a gully-field, whar dar was nuffin but bar' groun' an' hog weed. Now, dar was nuffin in dis worl' dat triflin' mule hated so much as hog weed, an' he says to hese'f : ' I's boun' ter do somefin' better'n dis fur a libin. I reckin I'll go skeer dat ole Harris, an' make him gib me a feed o' corn.' So he jump ober de fence, fur he was spry 'nuf when he had a min' ter, an' he steals an ole bar skin dat he'd seen hangin' up in de store po'ch, an' he pretty nigh kivered himse'f all up wid it. Den he go down to de pos' offis, whar de mail had jes' come in. When dis triflin' ole mule seed de cullud man, Harris, sittin' on de bottom step ob de po'ch, he begin to kick up his heels an' make all de noise he could wid he mouf. 'Wot's dat?' cried de cullud man, Harris. 'I's a big grizzly bar,' said de mule, ''scaped from de 'nagerie when 'twas fordin' Scott's Creek.' 'When did you git out?' said de cullud man, Harris. 'I bus' from de cage at half pas' free o'clock dis ebenin'. 'An' is you reely a grizzly bar?' 'Dat's de truf,' said de triflin' mule, 'an' I's pow'ful hungry, an' if you don' go git me a feed o' corn I'll swaller you down whole.' An' he begun to roar as like a grizzly bar as he knew how. 'Dat all de truf, you tellin' me?' de cullud man, Harris, ask. 'Dat's all true as I's libin',' says de triflin' mule. 'All right, den,' says de cullud man, Harris, 'if you kin come from de ford on Scott's Creek in a hour an' a half, you kin carry de mail jes' as well as any udder mule, an' I's gwine ter buy a big cart whip, an' make you do it. So take off dat bar skin, an' come 'long wid me.' So you see Brudder Gran'son," continued 'Bijah, "dar's dif'rent kinds ob truf, an' you's got ter be mighty 'ticklar wot kind you sticks ter."

"Git up," said Grandison to his drowsy horse, as he started him on another furrow.

PLAIN FISHING.

PLAIN FISHING.

"WELL, sir," said old Peter, as he came out on the porch with his pipe, "so you came here to go fishin'?"

Peter Gruse was the owner of the farm-house where I had arrived that day, just before supper-time. He was a short, strong-built old man, with a pair of pretty daughters, and little gold rings in his ears. Two things distinguished him from the farmers in the country round about: one was the rings in his ears, and the other was the large and comfortable house in which he kept his pretty daughters. The other farmers in that region had fine large barns for their cattle and horses, but very poor houses for their daughters. Old Peter's ear-rings were indirectly connected with his house. He had not always lived among those mountains. He had been on the sea, where his ears were decorated, and he had travelled a good deal on land, where he had ornamented his mind with many ideas which were not in general use in the part of his State in which he was born. His house stood a little back from the high road, and if a traveller wished to be entertained, Peter was generally willing to take him in, provided he had left his wife and family at home. The old man himself had no objection to wives and children, but his two pretty daughters had.

These young women had waited on their father and myself at supper-time, one continually bringing hot griddle cakes, and the other giving me every opportunity to test the relative merits of the seven different kinds of preserved fruit which, in little glass plates, covered the otherwise unoccupied spaces on the tablecloth. The latter, when she found that there was no further possible way of serving us, presumed to sit down at the corner of the table and begin her supper. But in spite of this apparent humility, which was only a custom of the country, there was that in the general air of the pretty daughters which left no doubt in the mind of the intelligent observer that they stood at the wheel in that house. There was a son of fourteen, who sat at table with us, but he did not appear to count as a member of the family.

" Yes," I answered, " I understood that there was good fishing hereabout, and, at any rate, I should like to spend a few days among these hills and mountains."

"Well," said Peter, "there's trout in some of our streams, though not as many as there used to be, and there's hills a plenty, and mountains too, if you choose to walk fur enough. They're a good deal furder off than they look. What did you bring with you to fish with?"

"Nothing at all," I answered. "I was told in the town that you were a great fisherman, and that you could let me have all the tackle I would need."

"Upon my word," said old Peter, resting his pipe-hand on his knee and looking steadfastly at me, "you're the queerest fisherman I've see'd yet. Nigh every year, some two or three of 'em stop here in the fishin' season, and there was never a man who didn't bring his jinted pole, and his reels, and his lines, and his hooks, and his dry-goods flies, and his whiskey-flask with a long strap to it. Now, if you want all these things, I haven't got 'em."

"Whatever you use yourself will suit me," I answered.

"All right, then," said he. "I'll do the best I can for you in the mornin'. But it's plain enough to me that you're not a game fisherman, or you wouldn't come here without your tools."

To this remark I made answer to the effect that, though I was very fond of fishing, my pleasure in it did not depend upon the possession of all the appliances of professional sport.

"Perhaps you think," said the old man, "from the way I spoke, that I don't believe them fellers with the jinted poles can ketch fish, but that ain't so. That old story about the little boy with the pin-hook who ketched all the fish, while the gentleman with the modern improvements, who stood alongside of him, kep' throwin' out his beautiful flies and never got nothin', is a pure lie. The fancy chaps, who must have ev'rythin' jist so, gen'rally gits fish. But for all that, I don't like their way of fishin', and I take no stock in it myself. I've been fishin', on and off, ever since I was a little boy, and I've caught nigh every kind there is, from the big jew-fish and cavalyoes down South, to the trout and minnies round about here. But when I ketch a fish, the first thing I do is to try to git him on the hook, and the next thing is to git him out of the water jist as soon as I kin. I don't put in no time worryin' him. There's only two animals in the world that likes to worry smaller creeturs a good while afore they kill 'em; one is the cat, and the other is what they call the game fisherman. This kind of a feller never goes after no fish that don't mind being ketched. He goes fur them kinds that loves their home in the water and hates most to leave it, and he makes it jist as hard fur 'em as he kin. What the game fisher likes is the smallest kind of a hook, the thinnest line, and a fish that it takes a good while to weaken. The longer the weak'nin' business kin be spun out, the more the sport. The idee is to let the fish think there's a chance fur him to git away. That's jist like the cat with her mouse. She lets the little creetur hop off, but the minnit he gits fur enough away, she jumps on him and jabs him with her claws, and then, if there's any game left in him, she lets him try again. Of course the game fisher could have a strong line and a stout pole and git his fish in a good sight quicker, if he wanted to, but that wouldn't be sport. He couldn't give him the butt and spin him out, and reel him in, and let him jump and run till his pluck is clean worn out. Now, I likes to git my fish ashore with all the pluck in 'em. It makes 'em taste better. And as fur fun, I'll be bound I've had jist as much of that, and more, too, than most of these fellers who are so dreadful anxious to have everythin' jist right, and think they can't go fishin' till they've spent enough money to buy a suit of Sunday clothes. As a gen'ral rule they're a solemn lot, and work pretty hard at their fun. When I work I want to be paid fur it, and when I go in fur fun I want to take it easy and cheerful. Now I wouldn't say so much agen these fellers," said old Peter, as he arose and put his empty pipe on a little shelf under the porch-roof, "if it wasn't for one thing, and that is, that they think that their kind of fishin' is the only kind worth considerin'. The way they look down upon plain Christian fishin' is enough to rile a hitchin'-post. I don't want to say nothin' agen no man's way of attendin' to his own affairs, whether it's kitchen-gardenin', or whether it's fishin,' if he says nothin' agen my way; but when he looks down on me, and grins at me, I want to haul myself up, and grin at him, if I kin. And in this case, I kin. I s'pose the house-cat and the cat-fisher (by which I don't mean the man who fishes for cat-fish) was both made as they is, and they can't help it; but that don't give 'em no right to put on airs before other bein's, who gits their meat with a square kill. Good-night. And sence I've talked so much about it, I've a mind to go fishin' with you to-morrow myself."

The next morning found old Peter of the same mind, and after breakfast he proceeded to fit me out for a day of what he called "plain Christian trout-fishin'." He gave me a reed rod, about nine feet long, light, strong, and nicely balanced. The tackle he produced was not of the fancy order, but his lines were of fine strong linen, and his hooks were of good shape, clean and sharp, and snooded to the lines with a neatness that indicated the hand of a man who had been where he learned to wear little gold rings in his ears.

"Here are some of these feather insects," he said, "which you kin take along if you like." And he handed me a paper containing a few artificial flies. "They're pretty nat'ral," he said, "and the hooks is good. A man who came here fishin' gave 'em to me, but I shan't want 'em to-day. At this time of year grasshoppers is the best bait in the kind of place where we're goin' to fish. The stream, after it comes down from the mountain, runs through half a mile of medder land before it strikes into the woods agen. A grasshopper is a little creetur that's got as much conceit as if his jinted legs was fish-poles, and he thinks he kin jump over this narrer run of water whenever he pleases; but he don't always do it, and then if he doesn't git snapped up by the trout that lie along the banks in the medder, he is floated along into the woods, where there's always fish enough to come to the second table."

Having got me ready, Peter took his own particular pole, which he assured me he had used for eleven years, and hooking on his left arm a good-sized basket, which his elder pretty daughter had packed with cold meat, bread, butter, and preserves, we started forth for a three-mile walk to the fishing-ground. The day was a favorable one for our purpose, the sky being sometimes over-clouded, which was good for fishing, and also for walking on a highroad; and sometimes bright, which was good for effects of mountain-scenery. Not far from the spot where old Peter proposed to begin our sport, a small frame-house stood by the roadside, and here the old man halted and entered the open door without knocking or giving so much as a premonitory stamp. I followed, imitating my companion in leaving my pole outside, which appeared to be the only ceremony that the etiquette of those parts required of visitors. In the room we entered, a small man in his shirt-sleeves sat mending a basket-handle. He nodded to Peter, and Peter nodded to him.

"We've come up a-fishin'," said the old man. "Kin your boys give us some grasshoppers?"

"I don't know that they've got any ready ketched," said he, "for I reckon I used what they had this mornin'. But they kin git you some. Here, Dan, you and Sile go and ketch Mr. Gruse and this young man some grasshoppers. Take that mustard-box, and see that you git it full."

Peter and I now took seats, and the conversation began about a black cow which Peter had to sell, and which the other was willing to buy if the old man would trade for sheep, which animals, however, the basket-mender did not appear just at that time to have in his possession. As I was not very much interested in this subject, I walked to the back-door and watched two small boys in scanty shirts and trousers, and ragged straw hats, who were darting about in the grass catching grass-hoppers, of which insects, judging by the frequent pounces of the boys, there seemed a plentiful supply.

"Got it full?" said their father, when the boys came in.

"Crammed," said Dan.

Old Peter took the little can, pressed the top firmly on, put it in his coat-tail pocket, and rose to go. "You'd better think about that cow, Barney," said he. He said nothing to the boys about the box of bait; but I could not let them catch grass-hoppers for us for nothing, and I took a dime from my pocket, and gave it to Dan. Dan grinned, and Sile looked sheepishly happy, and at the sight of the piece of silver an expression of interest came over the face of the father. "Wait a minute," said he, and he went into a little room that seemed to be a kitchen. Returning, he brought with him a small string of trout. "Do you want to buy some fish?" he said. "These is nice fresh ones. I ketched 'em this mornin'."

To offer to sell fish to a man who is just about to go out to catch them for himself might, in most cases, be considered an insult, but it was quite evident that nothing of the kind was intended by Barney. He probably thought that if I bought grasshoppers, I might buy fish. "You kin have 'em for a quarter," he said.

It was derogatory to my pride to buy fish at such a moment, but the man looked very poor, and there was a shade of anxiety on his face which touched me. Old Peter stood by without saying a word. "It might be well," I said, turning to him, "to buy these fish, for we may not catch enough for supper."

"Such things do happen," said the old man.

"Well," said I, "if we have these we shall feel safe in any case." And I took the fish and gave the man a quarter. It was not, perhaps, a professional act, but the trout were well worth the money, and I felt that I was doing a deed of charity.

Old Peter and I now took our rods, and crossed the road into an enclosed field, and thence into a wide stretch of grass land, bounded by hills in front of us and to the right, while a thick forest lay to the left. We had walked but a short distance, when Peter said : " I'll go down into the woods, and try my luck there, and you'd better go along up stream, about a quarter of a mile, to where it's rocky. P'raps you ain't used to fishin' in the woods, and you might git your line cotched. You'll find the trout'll bite in the rough water."

" Where is the stream ? " I asked.

" This is it," he said, pointing to a little brook, which was scarcely too wide for me to step across, "and there's fish right here, but they're hard to ketch, fur they git plenty of good livin' and are mighty sassy about their eatin'. But you kin ketch 'em up there."

Old Peter now went down toward the woods, while I walked up the little stream. I had seen trout-brooks before, but never one so diminutive as this. However, when I came nearer to the point where the stream issued from between two of the foot-hills of the mountains, which lifted their forest-covered heights in the distance, I found it wider and shallower, breaking over its rocky bottom in sparkling little cascades.

Fishing in such a jolly little stream, surrounded by this mountain scenery, and with the privileges

9

of the beautiful situation all to myself, would have been a joy to me if I had had never a bite. But no such ill-luck befell me. Peter had given me the can of grasshoppers after putting half of them into his own bait-box, and these I used with much success. It was grasshopper season, and the trout were evidently on the lookout for them. I fished in the ripples under the little waterfalls; and every now and then I drew out a lively trout. Most of these were of moderate size, and some of them might have been called small. The large ones probably fancied the forest shades, where old Peter went. But all I caught were fit for the table, and I was very well satisfied with the result of my sport.

About noon I began to feel hungry, and thought it time to look up the old man, who had the lunch-basket. I walked down the bank of the brook, and some time before I reached the woods I came to a place where it expanded to a width of about ten feet. The water here was very clear, and the motion quiet, so that I could easily see to the bottom, which did not appear to be more than a foot below the surface. Gazing into this transparent water, as I walked, I saw a large trout glide across the stream, and disappear under the grassy bank which overhung the opposite side. I instantly stopped. This was a much larger fish than any I had caught, and I determined to try for him.

I stepped back from the bank, so as to be out of sight, and put a fine grasshopper on my hook; then I lay, face downward, on the grass, and worked myself slowly forward until I could see the middle of the stream; then quietly raising my pole, I gave my grasshopper a good swing, as if he had made a wager to jump over the stream at its widest part. But as he certainly would have failed in such an ambitious endeavor, especially if he had been caught by a puff of wind, I let him come down upon the surface of the water, a little beyond the middle of the brook. Grasshoppers do not sink when they fall into the water, and so I kept this fellow upon the surface, and gently moved him along, as if, with all the conceit taken out of him by the result of his ill-considered leap, he was ignominiously endeavoring to swim to shore. As I did this, I saw the trout come out from under the bank, move slowly toward the grasshopper, and stop directly under him. Trembling with anxiety and eager expectation, I endeavored to make the movements of the insect still more natural, and, as far as I was able, I threw into him a sudden perception of his danger, and a frenzied desire to get away. But, either the trout had had all the grasshoppers he wanted, or he was able, from long experience, to perceive the difference between a natural exhibition of emotion and a histrionic imitation of it, for he slowly turned, and, with a few slight movements of his tail, glided back under the bank. In vain did the grasshopper continue his frantic efforts to reach the shore; in vain did he occasionally become exhausted, and sink a short distance below the surface; in vain did he do everything that he knew, to show that he appreciated what a juicy and delicious morsel he was, and how he feared that the trout might yet be tempted to seize him; the fish did not come out again.

Then I withdrew my line, and moved back from the stream. I now determined to try Mr. Trout with a fly, and I took out the paper old Peter Gruse had given me. I did not know exactly what kind of winged insects were in order at this time of the year, but I was sure that yellow butterflies were not particular about just what month it was, so long as the sun shone warmly. I therefore chose that one of Peter's flies which was made of the yellowest feathers, and, removing the snood and hook from my line, I hastily attached this fly, which was provided with a hook quite suitable for my desired prize. Crouching on the grass, I again approached the brook. Gaily flitting above the glassy surface of the water, in all the fancied security of tender youth and innocence, came my yellow fly. Backward and forward over the water he gracefully flew, sometimes rising a little into the air, as if to view the varied scenery of the woods and mountains, and then settling for a moment close to the surface, to better inspect his glittering image as it came up from below, and showing in his every movement his intense enjoyment of summer-time and life.

Out from his dark retreat now came the trout, and settling quietly at the bottom of the brook, he appeared to regard the venturesome insect with a certain interest. But he must have detected the iron-barb of vice beneath the mask of blitheful innocence, for, after a short deliberation, the trout turned and disappeared under the bank. As he slowly moved away, he seemed to be bigger than ever. I must catch that fish! Surely he would bite at something. It was quite evident that his mind was not wholly unsusceptible to emotions emanating from an awakening appetite, and I believed that if he saw·exactly what he wanted, he would not neglect an opportunity of availing himself of it. But what did he want? I must certainly find out. Drawing myself back again, I took off the yellow fly, and put on another. This was a white one, with black blotches, like a big miller moth which had fallen into an ink-pot. It was surely a conspicuous creature, and as I crept forward and sent it swooping over the stream, I could not see how any trout, with a single insectivorous tooth in his head, could fail to rise to such an occasion. But this trout did not rise. He would not even come out from under his bank to look at the swiftly flitting creature. He probably could see it well enough from where he was.

But I was not to be discouraged. I put on another fly; a green one with a red tail. It did not look like any insect that I had ever seen, but I thought that the trout might know more about such things than I. He did come out to look at it, but probably considering it a product of that modern æstheticism which sacrifices natural beauty to mediæval crudeness of color and form, he retired without evincing any disposition to countenance this style of art.

It was evident that it would be useless to put on any other flies, for the two I had left were a good deal bedraggled, and not nearly so attractive as those I had used. Just before leaving the house that morning, Peter's son had given me a wooden match-box filled with worms for bait, which, although I did not expect to need, I put in my pocket. As a last resort I determined to try the trout with a worm. I selected the plumpest and most comely of the lot; I put a new hook on my line; I looped him about it in graceful coils, and cautiously approached the water, as before. Now a worm never attempts to wildly leap across a flowing brook, nor does he flit in thoughtless innocence through the sunny air, and over the bright transparent stream. If he happens to fall into the water, he sinks to the bottom; and if he be of a kind not subject to drowning, he generally endeavors to secrete himself under a stone, or to burrow in the soft mud. With this knowledge of his nature I gently dropped my worm upon the surface of the stream, and then allowed him slowly to sink. Out sailed the trout from under the bank, but stopped before reaching the sinking worm. There was a certain something in his action which seemed to indicate a disgust at the sight of such plebeian food, and a fear seized me that he might now swim off, and pay no further attention to my varied baits. Suddenly there was a ripple in the water, and I felt a pull on the line. Instantly I struck; and then there was a tug. My blood boiled through every vein and artery, and

I sprang to my feet. I did not give him the butt; I did not let him run with yards of line down the brook; nor reel him in, and let him make another mad course up stream; I did not turn him over as he jumped into the air; nor endeavor, in any way, to show him that I understood those tricks, which his depraved nature prompted him to play upon the angler. With an absolute dependence upon the strength of old Peter's tackle, I lifted the fish. Out he came from the water, which held him with a gentle suction as if unwilling to let him go, and then he whirled through the air like a meteor flecked with rosy fire, and landed on the fresh green grass a dozen feet behind me. Down on my knees I dropped before him as he tossed and rolled, his beautiful spots and colors glistening in the sun. He was truly a splendid trout, fully a foot long, round and heavy. Carefully seizing him, I easily removed the hook from the bony roof of his capacious mouth thickly set with sparkling teeth, and then I tenderly killed him, with all his pluck, as old Peter would have said, still in him.

I covered the rest of the fish in my basket with wet plantain leaves, and laid my trout king on this cool green bed. Then I hurried off to the old man, whom I saw coming out of the woods. When I opened my basket and showed him what I had caught, Peter looked surprised, and, taking up the trout, examined it.

"Why, this is a big fellow," he said. "At first I thought it was Barney Sloat's boss trout, but it isn't long enough for him. Barney showed me his trout, that gen'rally keeps in a deep pool, where a tree has fallen over the stream down there. Barney tells me he often sees him, and he's been tryin' fur two years to ketch him, but he never has, and I say he never will, fur them big trout's got too much sense to fool round any kind of victuals that's got a string to it. They let a little fish eat all he wants, and then they eat him. How did you ketch this one?"

I gave an account of the manner of the capture, to which Peter listened with interest and approval.

"If you'd a stood off and made a cast at that feller, you'd either have caught him at the first flip, which isn't likely, as he didn't seem to want no feather flies, or else you'd a skeered him away. That's all well enough in the tumblin' water, where you gen'rally go fur trout, but the man that's got the true feelin' fur fish will try to suit his idees to theirs, and if he keeps on doin' that, he's like to learn a thing or two that may do him good. That's a fine fish, and you ketched him well. I've got a lot of 'em, but nothin' of that heft.

After luncheon we fished for an hour or two with no result worth recording, and then we started for home. A couple of partridges ran across the road some distance ahead of us, and these gave Peter an idea.

"Do you know," said he, "if things go on as they're goin' on now, that there'll come a time when it won't be considered high-toned sport to shoot a bird slam-bang dead. The game gunners will pop 'em with little harpoons, with long threads tied to 'em, and the feller that can tire out his bird, and haul him in with the longest and thinnest piece of spool thread, will be the crackest sportsman."

At this point I remarked to my companion that perhaps he was a little hard on the game fishermen.

"Well," said old Peter, with a smile on his corrugated visage, "I reckon I'd have to do a lot of talkin' before I'd git even with 'em, fur the way they give me the butt for my style of fishin'. What I say behind their backs I say to their faces. I seed one of these fellers once with a fish on his hook, that he was runnin' up an' down the stream like a chased chicken. 'Why don't you pull him in?' says I. 'And break my rod an' line?' says he. 'Why don't you have a stronger line and pole?' says I. 'There wouldn't be no science in that,' says he. ' If it's your science you want to show off,' says I, 'you ought to fish for mud eels. There's more game in 'em than there is in any other fish round here, and as they're mighty lively out of water you might play one of 'em fur half an hour after you got him on shore, and it would take all your science to keep him from reelin' up his end of the line faster than you could yourn.' "

When we reached the farm the old man went into the barn, and I took the fish into the house. I found the two pretty daughters in the large room, where the eating and some of the cooking was done. I opened my basket, and with great pride showed them the big trout I had caught. They evidently thought it was a large fish, but they looked at each other, and smiled in a way that I did not understand. I had expected from them, at least, as much admiration for my prize and my skill as their father had shown."

" You don't seem to think much of this fine trout that I took such trouble to catch," I remarked.

" You mean," said the elder girl, with a laugh, " that you bought of Barney Sloat."

I looked at her in astonishment.

" Barney was along here to-day," she said, "and he told about your buying your fish of him."

" Bought of him ! " I exclaimed, indignantly. " A little string of fish at the bottom of the basket I bought of him, but all the others, and this big one, I caught myself."

"Oh, of course," said the pretty daughter, "bought the little ones and caught all the big ones ! "

" Barney Sloat ought to have kept his mouth shut," said the younger pretty daughter, looking at me with an expression of pity. " He'd got his money, and he hadn't no business to go telling on people. Nobody likes that sort of thing. But this big fish is a real nice one, and you shall have it for your supper."

" Thank you," I said, with dignity, and left the room.

I did not intend to have any further words with these young women on this subject, but I cannot deny that I was annoyed and mortified. This was the result of a charitable action. I think I was never more proud of anything than of catching that trout ; and it was a good deal of a downfall to suddenly find myself regarded as a mere city man fishing with a silver hook. But, after all, what did it matter ?

The boy who did not seem to be accounted a member of the family came into the house, and as he passed me he smiled good-humoredly, and said : " Buyed 'em ! "

I felt like throwing a chair at him, but refrained out of respect to my host. Before supper the old man came out on to the porch where I was sitting. " It seems," said he, " that my gals has got it inter their heads that you bought that big fish of Barney Sloat, and as I can't say I seed you ketch it, they're not willin' to give in, 'specially as I didn't git no such big one. 'Tain't wise to buy fish when you're goin' fishin' yourself. It's pretty certain to tell agen you."

" You ought to have given me that advice before," I said, somewhat shortly. " You saw me buy the fish."

" You don't s'pose," said old Peter, " that I'm goin' to say anythin' to keep money out of my neighbor's pockets. We don't do that way in these parts. But I've told the gals they're not to speak another word about it, so you needn't give your mind no worry on that score. And now let's go in to supper. If you're as hungry as I am, there won't be many of them fish left fur breakfast."

That evening, as we were sitting smoking on the porch, old Peter's mind reverted to the subject of the unfounded charge against me. " It goes pretty hard," he remarked, " to have to stand

up and take a thing you don' like when there's
no call fur it. It's bad enough when there is a
call fur it. That matter about your fish buyin' re-
minds me of what happened two summers ago to
my sister, or ruther to her two little boys—or, more
correct yit, to one of 'em. Them was two cur'ous
little boys. They was allus tradin' with each
other. Their father deals mostly in horses, and
they must have got it from him. At the time I'm
tellin' of they'd traded everythin' they had, and
when they hadn't nothin' else left to swap they
traded names. Joe he took Johnny's name, and
Johnny he took Joe's. Jist about when they'd
done this, they both got sick with sumthin' or
other, the oldest one pretty bad, the other not
much. Now there ain't no doctor inside of twenty
miles of where my sister lives. But there's one
who sometimes has a call to go through that part
of the country, and the people about there is allus
very glad when they chance to be sick when he
comes along. Now this good luck happened to
my sister, fur the doctor come by jist at this time.
He looks into the state of the boys, and while
their mother has gone downstairs he mixes some
medicine he has along with him. ' What's your
name?' he says to the oldest boy when he'd done
it. Now as he'd traded names with his brother,

fair and square, he wasn't goin' back on the trade, and he said, ' Joe.' ' And my name's Johnny,' up and says the other one. Then the doctor he goes and gives the bottle of medicine to their mother, and says he : ' This medicine is fur Joe. You must give him a tablespoonful every two hours. Keep up the treatment, and he'll be all right. As fur Johnny, there's nothin' much the matter with him. He don't need no medicine.' And then he went away. Every two hours after that Joe, who wasn't sick worth mentionin', had to swallow a dose of horrid stuff, and pretty soon he took to his bed, and Johnny he jist played round and got well in the nat'ral way. Joe's mother kept up the treatment, gittin' up in the night to feed that stuff to him ; but the poor little boy got wuss and wuss, and one mornin' he says to his mother, says he : ' Mother, I guess I'm goin' to die, and I'd ruther do that than take any more of that medicine, and I wish you'd call Johnny and we'll trade names back agen, and if he don't want to come and do it, you kin tell him he kin keep the old minkskin I gave him to boot, on account of his name havin' a Wesley in it.' ' Trade names,' says his mother, ' what do you mean by that ? ' And then he told her what he and Johnny had done. ' And did you ever tell anybody about this ? ' says she.

'Nobody but Dr. Barnes,' says he. 'After that I got sick and forgot it.' When my sister heard that, an idee struck into her like you put a fork into an apple dumplin'. Traded names, and told the doctor! She'd all along thought it strange that the boy that seemed wuss should be turned out, and the other one put under treatment; but it wasn't fur her to set up her opinion agen that of a man like Dr. Barnes. Down she went, in about seventeen jumps, to where Eli Timmins, the hired man, was ploughin' in the corn. 'Take that horse out of that,' she hollers, 'and you may kill him if you have to, but git Dr. Barnes here before my little boy dies.' When the doctor come he heard the story, and looked at the sick youngster, and then says he: 'If he'd kept his mink-skin, and not hankered after a Wesley to his name, he'd a had a better time of it. Stop the treatment, and he'll be all right.' Which she did; and he was. Now it seems to me that this is a good deal like your case. You've had to take a lot of medicine that didn't belong to you, and I guess it's made you feel pretty bad; but I've told my gals to stop the treatment, and you'll be all right in the mornin.' Good-night. Your candle-stick is on the kitchen table."

For two days longer I remained in this neigh-

borhood, wandering alone over the hills, and up
the mountain-sides, and by the brooks, which
tumbled and gurgled through the lonely forest.
Each evening I brought home a goodly supply of
trout, but never a great one like the noble fellow
for which I angled in the meadow stream.

On the morning of my departure I stood on the
porch with old Peter waiting for the arrival of the
mail driver, who was to take me to the nearest
railroad town.

" I don't want to say nothin'," remarked the old
man, " that would keep them fellers with the
jinted poles from stoppin' at my house when they
comes to these parts a-fishin'. I ain't got no objections to their poles ; 'tain't that. And I don't
mind nuther their standin' off, and throwin' their
flics as fur as they've a mind to ; that's not it.
And it ain't even the way they have of worryin'
their fish. I wouldn't do it myself, but if they
like it, that's their business. But what does rile
me is the cheeky way in which they stand up and
say that there isn't no decent way of fishin' but their
way. And that to a man that's ketched more
fish, of more different kinds, with more game in
'em, and had more fun at it, with a lot less money,
and less tomfoolin' than any fishin' feller that ever
come here and talked to me like an old cat tryin'

10

to teach a dog to ketch rabbits. No, sir ; agen I say that I don't take no money fur entertainin' the only man that ever come out here to go a-fishin' in a plain, Christian way. But if you feel tetchy about not payin' nothin', you kin send me one of them poles in three pieces, a good strong one, that'll lift Barney Sloat's trout, if ever I hook him."

I sent him the rod ; and next summer I am going out to see him use it.

www.ingramcontent.com/pod-product-compliance
Lightning Source LLC
Chambersburg PA
CBHW021123020726
47500CB00003B/891